PENCER

THE GRANT BROTHERS SERIES Book 3

KATHI S. BARTON

WCP

World Castle Publishing, LLC
Pensacola, Florida

Copyright © Kathi S. Barton 2011
ISBN: 9781937593001
Library of Congress Catalogue Number 2011937305
First Edition World Castle Publishing, LLC September 1, 2011
http://www.worldcastlepublishing.com

Licensing Notes

Cover: Karen Fuller
Editor: Brieanna Robertson

DEDICATION

I would like to say thank you to all my family, friends and fans.

~CHAPTER ONE~

"Sometimes you just need a bit of courage during the morning hours, don't you?" Cait looked at the woman behind her who had spoken.

When she nodded at the six pack of beer in with Cait's purchases, Cait looked down at the woman's own beer. She saw that there was one missing and then saw it was in the woman's hand. It was barely nine-thirty in the morning.

"I don't drink," Cait told her. Not that she had to explain to her, but she did. "It's for the chili we're having for dinner."

"Well, I do. And there are times, like today, that I need to start drinking earlier and earlier. I don't think my nerves can take it if I had to wait until five. But like someone once said, it's five somewhere."

Cait walked out of the little store and to her bike, shaking her head. Small towns, she thought. She was about to swing her leg over the seat when she heard the tires of screams in protest.

Without a single thought to her own safety, Cait ran to the scene.

~~~

"Where is she? My daughter? They said that she was brought in by ambulance." Spencer was frantic. He had torn across town and could not remember a single thing about the drive. He hoped that he at least stopped when he was supposed to and didn't break too many laws on the way in.

"Come this way, Doctor Grant. She's fine. You'll frighten her if you go back looking like this. Take a deep breath." The nurse he knew from his brother's work here, but for the life of him, he could not place her name.

He wanted to snarl at her, to tell her that he was scared himself. His little girl was here and she was keeping her from him. When someone put their hand on his shoulder, he turned to snap at whoever it was, but found two of his brothers.

"How is she?" Devin said with a huge bear hug.

"I don't know. I just...could I please go find my little girl? I need to see her right now." He knew he was barely holding on to his temper, but he was not going to be able to do that much longer.

The nurse apparently saw something in his face and motioned for them to come around to the closed door behind her.

He could hear her before they got there. A woman's voice, full of laughter and humor, was talking and making jokes. At first, he could not imagine why they would be headed that way, then he heard her speaking again.

"Yeah, kid, I've never known anyone who cheated at checkers before. You're all right. I like you."

He threw back the curtain the nurse indicated and stopped dead. He was not sure what he had expected, but a woman standing there with a gun pointed at him was not where is head was. When Devin and Nicky bumped into him, he heard one of them say, "shit." Understatement if he had ever heard one.

"My daughter," was all he got out before Meggie, his precious little girl, was in his arms. She had leapt he would swear from the bed. Life was suddenly all right again.

"Are you all right? Oh, baby, let me look at you." Her hands were going a mile a minute and he finally had to close his larger ones over hers to slow her down so that he could hear what she was saying.

Meggie Grant was a vibrant, happy and beautiful six-year-old, and she was also a deaf mute. He hugged her again.

Spencer then turned to the woman who had put her gun away now and was backing away from them. He noticed a smear on her shirt, but didn't register what it was.

"She said that you saved her life. That you kept her from being run over by a truck that was going too fast." He had to close his eyes for a second, the terror of what Meggie had told him overwhelming. Then he looked at her again.

"Yeah, well...I've got to go. She's a good kid, but she cheats at checkers. Whoever taught her that bears watching during poker night, I think. The driver of the truck didn't mean any harm. Everyone is fine."

She backed away a couple more steps and Spencer glanced at his brothers who stepped behind her. Spencer stood and sat his daughter on the bed again as he walked toward her.

"I don't know how to thank you. But you pulled a gun on me, which means you had one while you were sitting with my daughter. I realize she said you saved her, but I don't know you. I would like to know who you are and why you're armed."

"Caitlynne O'Malley. I have a permit for it. I have to meet the doc now in the other room. Don't! You need to step back from me. I don't want to have to hurt anyone, but I will if you touch me," she warned them while raising her hands up, her palms out and fingers spread wide.

"No one wants to be hurt. You just need to explain to me why you have a gun, that's all. Then everyone will be happy. How did you get it past security anyway?"

She swayed slightly, but stiffened when Nicky started for her. When she glanced at his brother, Nicky stepped back another step.

"I'm going to reach my left hand into my left pocket and pull out my ID. That's where my weapon is, as well as an extra magazine or clip. I'll need to pull it out and I'll put it into my right hand first before I take out anything else. Everyone cool with that?"

Spencer nodded and his brothers backed away from her. She moved her hand very slowly to her pocket and pulled out a gun and a clip, just as she had said. She pulled it out and pinched between her thumb and finger on the butt of it. The clip as well as the weapon were transferred to her other hand.

"It's loaded and hot. By hot I mean there is a round in the chamber, but I'm not touching the trigger. There is no safety on this particular type of weapon so I can't place it anywhere to get my ID for you. I don't know you any better than you know me and I'm not leaving my weapon where you can get to it. I'm going to get my ID now."

He knew suddenly that she was a cop. And with that realization, it occurred to him that she had been acting purely on instinct when he came upon her without warning and threw back the curtain. She had protected Meggie once again.

"You're a cop. I'm sorry, Officer O'Malley. My mother will have a fit when she finds out that I didn't guess that first."

She didn't say anything, but handed him a flat, black wallet. He noticed there was no badge and looked at her name and information when he opened it. "Detective Caitlynne A. O'Malley — Chicago Police Department — Homicide." He handed it back to her and smiled.

"My name is Spencer Grant. These are my brothers..." He was suddenly cut off by a large, booming voice yelling down the corridor. He glanced at Cait when he heard her whisper, "Well fuck a duck and watch it waddle."

~CHAPTER TWO~

"Where the hell are you, girly? I swear to Christ...I can't leave you alone for ten damned minutes and you go and...where are you?" Paddy yelled again.

Cait looked at the three men and shuddered. "I'm so sorry," she whispered before she answered the voice that was getting closer and closer. "Here you loud mouthed Irishman. Wanna keep it down a bit? They can probably hear you back at the house," she yelled back to her uncle.

The curtain was tossed back so hard that three of the rings snapped off, leaving it hanging at an odd angle. Meggie smiled at the burly man, Cait noticed. He had that effect on most women, no matter what the age.

"Christ, girly. Scared me, you did. Doona do that to me again." Cait could see the tears welling in his eyes before he jerked her to him. She didn't have time to avoid him, and pain already pulsing through her made her whimper in response.

"Christ! Let go." She didn't know if it was her tone or the small step she took to steady herself but he immediately obeyed. But too quickly and she felt the floor move under her feet and the walls shift. Pain shot through her body and pulsed to life like a living, breathing thing.

Before she realized it, she was on the bed next to the little girl and people were shouting around her. Her vision swam round and round and she closed her eyes. Taking deep breaths — well, as deep as she could under the circumstances, she tried to center herself and manage the pain.

"Detective O'Malley? Could you please help me before this man hurts me or my brothers?"

Cait opened her eyes again and looked up at Meggie's dad. Her uncle had him in a head lock and rather than fight him, it looked as if Spencer was letting the shorter man hold him.

He was gorgeous, she thought, with the deepest blue eyes she had ever seen. His dark hair looked like he had been running his fingers through it all day and there was chalk dust on his jacket sleeves. His jacket was a good cut, but it looked rumpled like he had slept in it. And if his shoulders where half as broad as they looked, she wanted to wrap around him and hang on tight.

It was not often that she met a man that was much taller than her. Cait was just under six foot and slender. But Spencer looked to be around six foot four inches easily and was built like a man who worked hard rather than hit the gym three or more times a week. His skin tone was light, but she didn't think it was for any reason other than he did not spend a lot of time outside. If he did, he would be a beautiful, yummy golden brown.

"Oh, Christ, I hurt," she groaned when she tried to sit up, and nearly passed out when she leaned up on her elbows to regard the room again. "Uncle Paddy, I'm fine. Please let the man go. What the fuck is wrong with you? I'm not helpless." She noticed that four more people had joined the first group, three men and an older woman.

"Yeah? Say that to me when your shirt ain't covered in blood. Damn it, Caddy — did — do you have any idea what happened...what I thought when he...you're supposed to be relaxing, healing. Your captain called it rest and relaxation, remember? Doona look to me like you did much of that today." Uncle Paddy's voice cracked and emotion swam in his dark green eyes.

Cait tried to get up to go to her uncle to hug him when one of the newcomers, another handsome man, pushed her back on the bed. He gave her a stern look, one that she could recognize as someone who was used to people listening to him. She cocked a brow at him.

"I'm Doctor Grant. Let's have a look at this blood, shall we? I want to see what you've done," he said.

She grabbed her shirt when he went to pull it up. "No. I...the stitches are just pulled. I'd like to go home. I'll be quiet for the rest of the day."

She started to move up again when he pushed her firmly back. She was starting to get a little pissed. She hated bossy people almost as much — well, she didn't much care for people in general when she was in pain.

"You're a cop, right? When I want advice on how to arrest someone, I'll call you. Right now, I'm the authority on blood. Let go of the shirt so I can see or I'll call a nurse in, have you sedated, and cut if from you. Your choice, Detective."

She lay back down, but didn't let go of the hem. She would not normally give in so quickly, but she hurt and she still felt a little dizzy. But she couldn't let go, not just yet. She needed him to understand that this was a normal run of the mill wound.

"Doc, I've been shot. It's bad. Please clear these people out, especially the kid," she told him in a low, urgent voice.

She didn't open her eyes, but heard him tell everyone to give him a few minutes and then the sounds of movements. Without opening her eyes, she knew that at least two other people besides the doc and her were still here. Her uncle's cologne gave him away and the other was the nurse that had stepped in just after the commotion started.

"Go away, Uncle Paddy. Or I'll have the doc here show you my bra and underwear. I think the ones I put on today are black and lacy. Besides, you promised."

"Yeah, and you promised not to get hurt too. Caitlynne, I can't...I love you darlin', please don't die on your old man. I donna think I can lose another family member."

"I'm not going anywhere. I love you too. But you know that I couldn't let that little girl get hurt. Go on outside and I'll be out soon. Okay?" She felt the tears stream down her cheeks, but ignored them.

She felt him lean down and kiss her on the forehead and he left. Cait knew that he was upset, but if he saw her wounds, it would be too much for both of them. It was too much for her to even look at. She couldn't think what he would say if he knew the extent of her injuries.

The doctor's voice startled her from her thoughts. "When where you shot, Detective?"

"Twenty-three days ago. Don't tell my uncle where the shots are. He knows I was shot in the chest. He just isn't aware of where they entered. Please? He doesn't want to...he has a bad heart."

She knew the moment the doctor realized what she meant. There was a bullet hole one inch below her right breast, and there were two more over her left, right over where her heart was.

"You're lucky you're alive, as I'm sure you've been told. There are a lot of stitches pulled open. I'm going to have to have these repaired in the operating room because of how close they are to your heart. I don't want to take the chance of anything going wrong, you understand. But I'm afraid you're not going home tonight, maybe not even tomorrow. I'm sorry, Detective."

She nodded. She knew as soon as she had scooped that child up in her arms she had done damage to the area. She had felt them pull apart and blood begin to seep, running warm against her skin. But like she had told her uncle, she couldn't have let the little girl be run down.

Cait noticed the children when she came out of the store, but didn't think about what information was being filed in her mind the minute she saw it. Filing and cataloging information was a big part of what she did. It was why she was as good as she was at her job as a detective. She could see the entire scene as if she had taken a photograph of it and could pull it up.

There had been a pop machine to the immediate right when Cait came out of the store. The open parking lot was long and narrow with only pull in spaces that one could only get to from the main street, and there were three cars there besides her bike. On the other side of the lot was another building, this one older and brick. It looked to be some sort of gift shop. The main street, appropriately named Main Street, was barely two lanes wide, bracketed by sidewalks that small trees had been planted next to and into them. The walk went the entire length of the street.

The children, nine of them, had been tied together by a rope, each tiny wrist knotted at about four feet apart. They had been standing near the pole that held the awning to the store. It was where they had been tethered. The little girl Meggie was last and had the longest gap between her and the child before her of about nine feet. They were all standing there milling about and watching the people enter and leave the little store.

The tires braking is what Cait had heard first and saw the little girl standing in the middle of the road trying to pick up a cat that was running from her. She didn't react to the people screaming at her nor the car coming at her. Cait now realized it was because she had not heard either of them.

"Detective? Are you all right? I can't give you anything for the pain, at least not until the surgeon comes in and approves it. I'll assist, but he'll be the one calling the shots. Unless you have a doctor you'd like me to have called in for you."

"It's O'Malley, or Cait. Just stop calling me detective, please. No. No drugs. When do you think I'll be able to leave?"

"Let's get you in the operating room first, all right?" he said with a chuckle.

The guy has a nice laugh and a very nice voice. He even smelled good, but not as good as the one called Spencer. Too bad he was married, she thought.

The next hour was a semi blur. The police had had to come in and relieve her of her weapon. She, as a fellow officer, could not give her weapon to anyone under her in rank so the Chief of Police had come in personally to take it from her and give her a receipt.

A weird thought popped into her head and she thought the man may have been running for some sort of office by the way he walked around like a banty rooster. Cait could not help but laugh when he heard that camera crews could not come in and watch him disarm her.

"But she's a hero. We need to have coverage of her and me together. She saved the little Handy girl."

"Right, and the little girl's name is not Handy and I said no. O'Malley needs to rest and you are taking up a lot of her airspace just by being here. Leave or I'll call security." Cait decided she might like Doctor Grant more and more all the time.

Her uncle and Aunt Deirdre came in to see her, but they had already started Cait's IV, so she was slightly out of it, but did remember seeing them. She made arrangements with her uncle about her weapon and he agreed. They stayed with her until she was wheeled into operating room three.

The last thing she remembered was the oxygen mask being sealed over her face and a small twinge of panic.

~CHAPTER THREE~

Spencer watched her chest move up and down without really seeing it. That would have surprised him had he thought about it. He loved a woman's breasts almost as much as he loved their laughter. He was so lost in thought that he barely registered the sound of squeaky shoes of the nurses going down the hall.

Meggie had gone home with his brother Nicky and his family. Spencer had stayed at the hospital with Damon to watch over the beautiful woman. He wanted to be there when she woke up. Paddy had taken Dee home because she didn't like hospitals and was becoming nervous.

He glanced down at the file on his lap Devin had dropped off thirty minutes ago and asked him to read. He had. He was having a hard time equating the woman in the file with the woman on the bed.

Caitlynne Alexandra O'Malley was twenty-nine and worked as a homicide detective for the Chicago PD. She had been working since graduating from the

Academy at twenty. She had worked her way up by hard work and a good nose for crime solving. Then four weeks ago, her partner had shot her and she returned fire, killing him and two other officers in an altercation at the firing range. She was on paid medical leave pending investigation. When she had been released from the hospital a week ago, her uncle, Patrick Shawn O'Malley, retired detective himself, had been there to bring her back to his home in Ohio. She was to rest and relax and under no circumstances was she to lift anything near the weight of his daughter.

Devin didn't know what had happened at the shooting as the details were being held until Internal Affairs finished their investigation. But he had said that she was lucky to be alive and that this was not the first time she had been called under review. She had always come out on top and had never been on the take.

Spence looked up at her when she moaned and he saw that she was looking at him. He smiled at her. She was very pretty even with her hair pulled up under an ugly cap and tubes running from under her gown.

"You should go home. This is no place for you to be when your wife and daughter need you. My uncle will be back soon anyway."

Her voice was scratchy and low and he rolled his chair closer to her bed to hear her better.

"Meggie is with my brother and his wife and I'm not married. Are you?" He didn't know why he had asked when he had all that information in front of him. But he wanted to hear her say it to be sure.

"No. Not married. Men find out I carry a gun and a badge, they tend to run in the other direction or they think I like to play rough. I usually shoot those guys in the nuts." She chuckled and moaned at the same time. "Did the doc say when I can go home?"

Spencer reached up and moved her hair from her eyes and smiled. "No, but he did say you have the loveliest breasts he has ever seen. And being a doctor, he has seen a lot of them."

"Ah, men are usually turned off when they see I have three nipples on one of my breasts and none on the other." He must have looked shocked because she laughed and said, "I'm kidding, Grant."

He felt drawn to her and didn't know why. Actually, he found he didn't care, not really. He realized that he had been wrong when he had said she was pretty. She was beautiful in a way that he had never really thought of before, simple. Her hair was bright red, carroty; he supposed he had heard it called. Her skin was milky white, but not unhealthy, with freckles everywhere including two on her lower lip. And her lips, Spencer thought, were enough to make a grown man whimper and think all sorts of carnal thoughts. He thought about how they would taste and noticed a small scar in the middle of her upper one.

"My first name is Spencer. How did you get this scar here? Some bad guy take exception to you arresting him?" He ran his thumb over the tiny mark that he had only noticed because he was so close to her. His voice had lowered and become huskier, his mouth dry too.

"No, nothing so nefarious as that. Our precinct was playing against fire for the championship two summers ago. I was first baseman and a guy came at me full tilt trying to get a base out of a foul ball. I caught it and he was a little...pissed that I had the nerve to catch it. Grant, you really need to back up a little bit. You're really crowding my space."

"My first name is Spencer. What did he hope to gain by running on a foul? Wouldn't he have been better off just taking the strike?" Leaning forward more, he was now only an inch or two from her mouth, where he wanted to be in the worst way.

"Maybe, but the fact that I had hit a homer in the inning before off his pitch had him trying for a little revenge. He had thrown a no hitter for three straight games prior to that. And I know your first name. Do you plan to kiss me, Grant?"

"Say my name, Caitlynne. I want to hear you say it." He brushed his lips over hers, barely touching them, then moved back a couple of inches.

"Not until we are in the throes of passion and you've made me come several times already. And I don't see that happening anytime too soon, do you, Grant?"

"Oh, yes. I do, as a matter of fact. Very soon." And he closed his mouth over hers.

He thought to only kiss her briefly, to press his mouth to hers and pull back. But the moment he touched her, his body had other ideas in mind. And when she opened her mouth under the gentle probe of his tongue, he knew he could not pull back even if his life depended on it. He was quite sure that even then might be a problem.

She tasted sweet, like the lemony swab they had pressed in her mouth when she came back from surgery, but sweeter. Her mouth was hot and wet, her tongue was quick, and when it moved along his, swirling around it, he could feel it as if she was licking along his cock.

He was glad he was sitting down because he was sure that every drop of blood in his body had pooled in his groin, making him harder than he could ever remember being. Reaching up, he cupped the back of her head and tilted her a little and deepened the kiss more, darting in and out of her mouth in much the same way he wanted to be doing to her with his body. A moment of shock rushed through him. Never had he had those thoughts about someone he had just met. But then, he only wanted to taste and keep on tasting.

Bells, he could swear he heard bells. He had kissed quite a few women in his lifetime and he could honestly say he had never heard bells before. But before he could think too much on that, he found himself still sitting in the chair, but several feet away from her bed. There were several people now where he had been and they did not look overly happy to see either of them.

He was grinning again. He had been since Damon had pulled him into his office ten minutes ago to yell at him. Spencer knew this because Damon was glaring at him. Again. But he couldn't seem to help himself. He was happy and not even his brother giving him a good dressing down could dampen that mood.

"Do you have any idea how stressful it is to the men and women who respond to a Code Blue? They have to move quickly and have everything in place before they go into a room. Every instrument, every med has to be ready—they have to be...this is serious, Spencer! What the hell were you thinking?"

"That she tasted too good to stop. That if I did have to stop, then I was going to enjoy it as much as I could. Christ, Damon, lighten up. Everyone in her room thought it was great."

They had actually congratulated them both on making the heart monitor register she had been hooked up to pop a fuse. They said that they had never responded to a Code Blue and been so happy to see that it was nothing.

"That is not the point! What if it had been a real emergency? Huh? What would you have done then?"

"I don't believe I would have been enjoying having my mouth over hers quite so much if it had been. I'm sorry, Damon. Sorry if I embarrassed you, but not for kissing her. And if you're quite through yelling at me, I think I'll go back to her room and try and blow up another one."

"She's asleep. The nurse checked her vitals when she was in there and Detective O'Malley asked for a pain pill. Apparently when they tore you from her, they pulled her arm too and hurt her. Spencer, you know nothing about this girl and she just saved your daughter. Maybe it's nothing more than that, gratitude."

Spencer turned on his brother in the next heartbeat. He had never been so angry so quickly in his life. He started stalking toward him and saw his reflection in the mirror behind Damon. That stopped him cold. He didn't just look angry, but crazy mad. He opened his mouth to say something and knew that whatever spewed from his mouth, most of it he would regret.

"Don't talk to me right now. I'm going to see O'Malley, and then I'm going home. If you call me before I call you, don't expect me to answer you. Good night."

Spencer went to Caitlynne's room and looked down at her. She was more beautiful every time he saw her and he wanted to see more of her. Grinning, he thought of her saying his name, his first name, and could not wait to get them both to that point of passion. Leaning down, he kissed her gently. Then he reluctantly left her so that he could get some sleep, hoping he could think about her when he did. Oh yeah, he thought, he was really looking forward to her saying his first name. Over and over and over again.

~~~

Cait woke to a semi darkened room. She knew she was in the hospital, so that did not frighten her, but the man in her room did. Very slowly, she reached down for the nurse call button.

"If someone comes in before I'm ready to leave, they'll be as dead as your partner. I'm here on behalf of a very concerned citizen. You'll listen, make a wise decision, and then everyone will be happy. Got it?"

"Fuck you. Tell Martinez that I said he's going down. Now get out of my room before I put you in the morgue."

He stalked to her bed and reached into his jacket as he went. She had her weapon drawn and centered on his chest before he took two steps. He stopped all movement; including his movement toward what Cait had assumed was a gun.

"Take your hands and put them on your head; lock your fingers. You do anything more than that and I will shoot you, have no doubt." She pulled the cord to the station and prayed someone was there and would act without asking too many questions. Within seconds, someone answered. "This is Detective O'Malley in room two-seventeen; I need you to call the police immediately. Tell them officer needs assistance, to send help."

There was no reply right away and Cait had a sudden feeling that her man had not come alone and someone else had taken care of the nurse. She was nearly out of the bed when the nurse came back.

"They are on their way, Detective. They said to hang tight. I've called hospital security too and they are on their way as well."

"Tell them not to enter until they hear from me. I want you to write this down as I give it to you, and then relay it to the police dispatcher." Cait was near the man now, adrenaline surging through her body. She knew she should have been in pain, and knew that she would pay when this was over. Reaching into the man's jacket, she pulled out his weapon by her two fingers, and tossed it on the bed just behind her. "Male Caucasian, dark hair, black shirt, black jacket, black pants and shoes, approximate age mid-thirties, height about six-three, weight two-forty, tat on left hand, a tear drop, could be a part of Martinez goon patrol. Got it?"

"Yes, Detective. This line will be open and I will stand by. Please don't hurt yourself. Doctor Grant will be sorely pissed if you do. He has been notified as well."

Cait did not answer, but backed two steps away from her man. She was slightly dizzy and her arm was aching. Gripping the footboard, she kept her gun trained on the man standing before her.

"You'll regret this. You should just quit now while you're ahead." He snarled at her. She didn't tell him that she already was, but she doubted that they were talking about the same thing.

"In case you hadn't noticed, I have a gun on you. Now, shut up and go down on your knees, a position you should maybe get used to, by the way. I'm not shitting you about a false move. I have no problem killing you."

Guiding him to the floor with her hand gripping his fingers on his head, he didn't go down gently. She then put her gun to the back of his head and had him lower himself to the floor, face to the side. When his hands were back on his head and fingers locked, she stepped back and heard the first knock at the door.

"Hospital security here, Detective O'Malley. May we come in?"

"Hang on a sec," she shouted at the closed door. Then to the man on the floor, she continued with her search. "Take your left foot and cross it to the back of your right leg at your knee, then lift you right foot up and stay that way." Once he had complied, she knelt down and put all her weight against his upright leg, holding him into a pretzel like position.

From this position on the floor, not only could he not move, but he couldn't throw her off either. Putting her gun in his back, she lifted his jacket and took out another gun and three extra clips. There was also a wallet, which only had cash inside and a knife in a sheath on his right leg. She couldn't reach his pant pockets like this, but she knew he couldn't either.

"When you come in, come in one at a time or I'll shoot whoever comes in behind you, you understand?" Cait shouted to the door. While she didn't take her eyes off her would-be murderer, she could see who or what came in the door in the mirror.

"Yes, ma'am, one at a time. I'm coming in now." Cait watched as the man came in slowly, his hands over his head, showing her he had nothing in them. She almost laughed; poor kid looked ready to wet his pants.

"You armed?" He nodded. "Good. How many others are out there with you?"

"Two, ma'am. You know you're not supposed to have a gun while in the hospital, right? It's against company policy and you can get into real trouble for it."

"If I didn't have it, I'd be dead right now. This guy wasn't coming in to wish me a speedy recovery. And stop calling me ma'am. Its Detective or Cait, but not ma'am. I'm not your flipping mother. Hand me those cuffs, please. And then let one of your cohorts in. One! Understand?"

"Yes, ma...Okay, Detective." He went to the door and let the next guy in and Cait did chuckle. She knew she was only twenty-nine, but this kid looked fresh out of middle school. Once he was clear of the door, the third guy was let in.

"I'm going to step off this man and I want you three to move back. If he moves, I don't want to accidently shoot one of you if I don't have to. It would be a real shame if that happened."

"Yeah, I like that plan. I'd just soon not be dead if it's all the same to you, Detective." The second guy nodded sagely. She decided that she needed a break at that moment. Maybe a long vacation where people were not trying to kill her, she thought, would be nice.

The police sirens could be heard getting closer. Within three minutes, four police entered her room and took charge of her man. Her uncle Paddy arrived within five minutes of the police. Uncle Paddy looked at her, but said nothing. She could see the terror and relief on his face.

She was back in bed when Damon arrived and was being examined by him when Spencer rushed in. Her room resembled a squad room, including bad coffee and filthy jokes. She was laughing at one when Spencer walked over to her bed. She noticed that he did not look like a happy man. Well, neither was she. She had been having a nice nap when this idiot had walked in.

"Hey guys, why don't we take this up later? I think you have all you need, right? I'm thinking I need to rest up before the doc blows a gasket," Cait suggested to the room.

"Course, O'Malley. Why don't you all go on home? I gotta ask the pretty little detective here a few questions." When the room cleared, the captain turned to her again. "Wanna tell me where you got that piece first? When you do, I'll be happy to go on my merry way too," Captain Donald Tucker asked her as he leaned at the foot of her bed.

"I have no idea what you're talking about. I handed my gun over to your chief a few hours ago. I believe you were here when I did," she told him with all innocence.

"Man with the hospital security said that when he came in, you had a Glock pointed at the perp's head and that you had him in a pretty lock down pose. You don't 'spect me to believe that he just dropped down like that 'cause you batted your pretty violet eyes at him, do you?"

"Are you saying that I'm not charming enough to have a man do anything I asked him to? Captain Tucker, you wound me. And here I thought you and I had a special moment there."

Captain Tucker looked over at her uncle, then back at her. She did not need to look at Uncle Paddy to know that he gave nothing away. They both knew that if anyone found out he had given her another gun not ten minutes after she came out of surgery, he would be in hot water. But she also knew that he could look as innocent as she could — she had learned the trick from him. He was another one she did not play poker with.

"And if I tossed that bed of yours, what would I find?" Captain Tucker asked as he pointed to the sheet now draped over her feet. He was careful not to touch her or the bed.

Instead of answering him, she moved to the side and slid out of the bed even as Doctor Grant hissed his disapproval. She moved over a foot, far enough away to let him search, but not far enough to let go of the bed. She was dizzy, but not stupid.

Captain Tucker started toward the head of the bed without breaking eye contact with her. He stopped just short of touching it. She knew what he was doing; first to blink lost.

"I toss that bed and find a gun; there'll be hell to pay. I toss that bed and there ain't anything, there'll be hell to pay. Why don't you tell me that you are going to behave yourself until you get out of here and I'll give us both a break?"

"The only thing I can honestly tell you, Captain, is that I will try to behave while I'm here. As soon as arrangements can be made, I'm heading back to Chicago anyway. I kind of think I've worn out my welcome."

"They gonna protect you there, or they gonna lead you to the wolves?" he asked after a few seconds.

Cait didn't answer. They both knew the answer to that. If Martinez could get her here, then what was to stop him from getting to her in his own town?

"Yeah, that's what I thought. You stay here, kid. If'n you want to transfer here, then I'll take you. Can always use a good detective, even if you are a female and a pain in my ass already. You maybe should take care of this boyfriend of yours too. He looks ready to bust a gut."

"Thanks, Captain. I'll keep that in mind. And this isn't high school and he's not my anything. Get out before I tell your wife you had a Tommy's sub for dinner." With a quick wink, he turned on his heel and left. She was so relieved that she took several breaths before getting back into the bed.

"You know that most patients of mine who just get out of surgery listen to my advice and stay in bed and rest. I can see that you need a lesson in that. Detective O'Malley, you're just lucky that I don't have to put you back under again. You need to stay in bed or I'll have to sedate you until such time that you can heal."

"Hummm, maybe. But you do that and I'll be dead. I'm in the middle of a few things that require me to be alert and aware. If you'd like, I can find myself a new doc."

He looked at her for a few seconds, then at his brother. Cait knew what he was thinking. Maybe he should let her, but in the end, he just shook his head.

"No, that won't be necessary. I'll hang around until you're on the mend. But we do need to have at least some sort of working relationship. I ask you to say in bed and you try to do it. What do you think?"

"Sure. I'll try. Thanks, doc. You might want to turn your head, I have to...my uncle needs to retrieve something."

"Shit, girly, I thought for sure the gig was up when he walked to the bed. Good thinking, you, getting outa the bed like that. Did you take the piece out with you?" Uncle Paddy asked, relief in his voice too.

"Uncle Paddy, what was the point of my telling them to turn their heads if you're going to...never mind. Just take it and put it in your coat. If someone else comes in now, I'll have to take my chances." She tossed the pillow to the end of the bed and showed him where the gun was hidden. She didn't even look at either of the Grants as she got into the bed.

~CHAPTER FOUR~

Spencer watched as Paddy picked up the gun and put it in the back of his pants as if it was an everyday thing. Maybe it was to him, but not to Spencer. He was dizzy with the implications of what her needing the gun had meant. And what she needed it for.

He knew Caitlynne was a cop, and he knew that the police carried guns, but he had never thought about them actually using them, or being shot by them. He looked at her. She had been shot and had she not had the weapon tonight—one she was not supposed to have—she would more than likely be dead.

"Leave her the gun."

"What! Are you insane? I won't have a gun in my hospital. Just knowing that she had one is bad enough. What if it had gone off and killed an innocent bystander? What then? No, no gun." Damon crossed his arms over his chest and stared at the three of them.

"If she didn't have the gun, he would have killed her and anyone else that would have gotten in his way while he was coming in or out of this building. Do you know how many people he could have taken out? You said he had extra clips, how many bullets is that?" Spencer turned to Cait and asked her suddenly.

"There are fifteen in each clip; he had three of them. So forty-five give or take."

She slid into the bed and waited to see where this was going. She wanted the gun. Spencer was right; she would have been killed if she had not had it.

"Forty-five dead people, Damon. Not just her, but others. Patients, staff — hell, you could have been a part of his spree. What if Mom...I don't even want to think about that."

"You should realize that there are the fifteen in the clip that was in the gun. Plus, there would be an extra one in the muzzle. That makes it sixty plus. And he would have killed them too. He would have used them all as a way to distract the police so he could escape. And his type will escape, even if he had to hide behind someone while he did it," she said.

Spencer could tell his brother was torn. If he left her the gun, then he was going against everything he had been taught, his oath to keep people healthy. If he took the gun from her and someone came back for her and killed even one person, including her, he would never be able to forgive himself.

"I don't want one single person in this hospital to know about this. If they find out, I'm going to say I knew nothing about any of this. Deal?"

"Thank you, doc, you're all right." The gun was tucked back under the pillow and Cait was helped back in over it. After a few more minutes of conversation, everyone left but Spencer.

Spencer wanted to talk to Cait about what had happened. He also wanted to bring her into his arms and hold her there, but for some reason, he thought that she would hurt him if he tired. She didn't strike him as the cuddly type. Before he could decide if it would be worth the pain, she started talking.

"You left this here the last time you were here." She threw the gray file at him that his brother had given him when she had first come in. Well, shit.

"I can explain. My brother gave it to me. He said that he thought I should know what kind of person was hanging out with my daughter." He cringed when he thought about the way that had come out.

"Hanging with your daughter? Does he have precognitive powers? Because the only time I was hanging with your daughter was when I scooped her up out from in front of a truck, then here in the hospital. Well, I can see where that would terrify you and him. Tell me, does he know if I make it back home to Chicago? Or if I live through the trial? Information like that would be really helpful. Especially in my line of work."

"It's not like that. He was just being thorough. He is...we all are very protective of Meggie. We don't want anyone to hurt her."

She was so quiet that he was nervous. He wasn't worried about the gun she carried; he was worried she would not see him again. Which, when he thought about it, was just plain stupid.

"I would never hurt a child, but I thank you for thinking I would. I'm going home to Chicago as soon as I'm released from here. I would very much like it if you stayed the hell away from me from now on. I'll also release your brother from him being my doctor as well. That way I don't contaminate anyone else in your family. Now, get out."

"Caitlynne, please don't do this. I'm so sorry. This isn't how…"

"Get the fuck out of here."

He left. But he was not finished. Not yet. His first stop was to his brother Devin's office.

"You are going to the hospital and fix this, or I fix you. She won't talk to me because you gave me that fucking file," he said as soon as he opened the office door.

"What are you talking about?" Spencer watched his brother stuffing files in his briefcase. He looked…Spencer thought he looked worried.

"O'Malley. She won't speak to me because you…what the hell is wrong with you? You look, I don't know, upset. Did she call you and cuss you out? Wouldn't surprise me if she did; she's spunky like that."

"Spunky? Where do you hang out? Never mind, I have a case. I don't know, something about it doesn't…I'll talk to her. I have to go talk to her about her report to the police about Ms. Ames. The detective told the police that she thought Meggie's teacher was drinking prior to the incident. There was something about an open container in the store."

"Drinking? It was nine o'clock in the morning. Is she sure? Wait, of course she is, and you know it, don't you? What's going on, Devin? What aren't you telling me?"

"Let me talk to your girlfriend first, all right? Then I'll get back to you. I should be done in time for dinner. Why don't you meet me at the hospital in a couple of hours, all right? Then you and I will have some dinner."

Spencer was not happy about it, but he didn't want to add anymore pressure on his brother right now. He decided that he would talk to his other brother, Nicky, and see if he knew anything.

~~~

Cait was dozing when her door opened. She had her weapon on her lap and when she realized she didn't know the man standing there, she slipped her fingers along its butt and curved them around it. Her index finger moved along the muzzle to just outside the trigger guard.

"Detective O'Malley. My name is Devin Grant. I'm the brother of Damon and Spencer Grant. May I come in?" the man said. She could see the resemblance, but that didn't matter.

"I'm sorry about your family, Mr. Grant. It's too bad you can't pick your family like you can friends. You have ID? And if so, then you take it out slowly and no one gets hurt. I have a gun pointed at your chest and I'm too pissed off at your brothers to care if you die or not."

She wouldn't really shoot him for being Spencer's brother, but he didn't have to know that. She didn't bring up her weapon. At this point she could kill him without any problem if he was not who he said he was.

Cait watched as he sat his briefcase down and opened his jacket and reached into it slowly. He was moving slower than slow and if the circumstances were not so grave, she might have laughed at him.

"I'm an attorney. The police called to let me know that you had filed a report against Ms. Ames. I received a copy of it as I'm representing my brother and the other parents in this matter. I'd like to talk to you about it, if you don't mind."

She took the wallet that he had opened for her and read his driver's license. When she was satisfied that he was telling her the truth, she handed it back to him.

"What do you want to know?" He handed her the file. She opened it and a photo slipped into her lap. She studied it for a few seconds and held it up. "What does a murdered vic have to do with a school teacher?"

"What? Shit. Sorry, I must have put it...suicide. Here, let me put that back in the correct one."

"Murdered. The teacher was drinking in the store. The girl at the register, Holly, was giving her what-for because the teacher opened one in the store. She also spoke to me about needing to start drinking earlier every day for her nerves."

"Did you see her...why do you think William was murdered?" He brought the picture back out of his case and was staring at it. He looked very much like Spencer when he frowned like that, and she smiled.

"I don't think it; he was. Why do you think he wasn't? Because unless you actually saw him do it, then I'm right; it's murder. I've seen this more times than you. I know the difference." She was not being arrogant; she was stating facts.

"He left a note. His wife and friends said he had been depressed lately. When I talked to him a few weeks ago, he was disturbed about something too."

"I'm sure that last night I would have left a note too if the guy who came in here had succeed in killing me. Staging is everything to these guys. A note does not a suicide make, Mr. Grant. He was murdered. There are all sorts of clues if one just knows what to look for."

"My name is Devin. Mr. Grant was my father. Show me. I'm sorry. This case has not...William was a good friend and this hasn't set well with me for several days. He contacted me several weeks ago and told me that he was having problems with money, but he didn't say they were bad, just problems. He said that if anything were to happen to him, that I and only I was to sign off on his death. I just don't...he was...I'm sorry. Could you tell me what you see?"

Cait could tell that he was upset, so she decided to tell him. She didn't need the picture; she had committed it to memory. Lying back on the bed, she decided to help him, but to help him figure it out as well.

"Give me your hand and help me up." She didn't reach until he held out his hand. When he had, she held on. "Now, what time is it?" She watched as the extended his left arm to pull his sleeve back to see his watch. "Stop!"

He stared at her, waiting. She had to hand it to him; he followed direction very well. Laughing, she said, "Look at your hands and tell me what you see. And don't think too hard on it; just tell me."

He looked at both of his hands, one still tight in hers, the other extended just beyond. She knew he would get it sooner or later, but decided to help him. "You handed me your hand. Why this one?"

"You reached for it...wait, no you didn't. Let's see. I handed you my right hand...I handed you my right hand because I'm right-handed and it's my dominant hand." He seemed pleased. She was as well.

"And your other hand, what are you seeing there?" She didn't look at his watch; she knew that he would understand.

"My watch. I have my watch on my left so that...so that...I have no idea. It's just the wrist I put it on when I wake up every morning." He smiled at her it made him look like a kid with his hand in the cookie jar.

"Yes, you do, Mr. Grant. Why would you put your watch on your less dominant wrist?"

"Devin. So that when I need to tell some detective trying to make a point what time it is, I will have a free hand? I have no idea."

"Yes and no. You use your right hand more, say for writing or holding a cup of coffee. Whatever. But if you needed to tell some stupid detective the time, you'd do what you just did."

"Okay, what does this have to...shit! William was left-handed." He picked up the picture that he had laid on her bed.

The picture showed a man with the left side of his head lying on a desk. He was facing the camera. There was blood pooled under his head and a hole in his right temple, the coroner had said. The gun, a Glock, was lying next to him; his hand was slightly wrapped around the butt of it. Two fingers of his right hand were still inside the trigger guard.

"He would have used his left and the wound would have been on the left as well. He wouldn't have shot himself with his less dominant hand, would he?"

"No. Not normally. It could happen, I suppose, if he were ambidextrous. But that isn't all, Mr. Grant. His head was placed on the desk. And his hand is not holding the gun correctly, in addition to it being in the wrong hand. All that adds up to murder, not suicide. I'm guessing that he had a typed note and that there wasn't a signature either."

"Call me Devin. What do you mean about his head?"

~CHAPTER FIVE~

Spencer walked in and watched as Cait was standing behind Devin. He was sitting in a chair and she was holding his head with one of her hands. Spencer sat down. It was either that or beat his brother to a bloody pulp for being this close to her.

"Okay, Mr. Grant, now put your right finger to your head as if you are going to shoot yourself. I'm not going to hurt you, but just demonstrate the impact, well, slightly demonstrate. The only way to get the true affect it for me to shoot you. But that would be messy and too much paperwork."

Devin put his finger to his head, made a pop noise, and Cait snapped his head to the left hard with her right hand. He noticed she favored her left. He winced when his brother looked to be in pain. Then smiled. Okay, this was not so bad if she could hurt Devin for him.

"Your head would never drop to the desk all pretty like in the picture. If anything, the impact from the Glock at a range of that close, he would have been lucky not to have been thrown to the floor. A Glock does not make a good suicide weapon. You need to use a revolver."

"Christ. William was murdered. I have to...you have no idea what you've done for me." Devin jumped up, reached behind the chair, pulled her toward him and kissed her full on the mouth.

Spencer jumped up just as Cait stepped back. He didn't move; she looked not just shocked, but angry too.

"I'm sorry. I was...I didn't think. Spence, I'm sorry. I have to go. I have a few calls to make. Thank you, Cait. I will talk to you tomorrow about the teacher. You can't leave town until I do. I'll serve you if I have to."

"I helped you and you are pulling this shit? Wow, you are a Grant, aren't you? I won't leave, but don't count on anymore help from me."

"Fine, so long as you are here to answer questions and to go to trial if need be. I appreciate your help. And as for Spencer, he had nothing to do with the file he had on you. That was totally me. Have a good night."

Spencer straightened up and walked to her as his brother left. She looked pissed and glared at him. He grinned. She was beautiful and he wanted to taste her again.

"You aren't supposed to be here. I think I've made myself perfectly clear on that point...back up, Grant. I'm not kidding. You're in my space again and I've warned you enough."

He stalked her, pressing her back as he advanced. She hit the wall; he bracketed her with his hands on either side of her. He was inches away from her and he could still feel her heat.

"My brother got a kiss. Where is mine?" Spencer nuzzled her neck and nipped at the tight muscle there. Running his tongue along her throat, he pulled her ear lobe into his mouth and suckled it. She tasted better today then she had two days ago when he had kissed her.

"He took his...back off, Grant. I'm serious." She put her hands up to his chest, but he didn't feel her press him back. In fact, she curled her fingers into his chest. He leaned closer. Heat pooled between them, from both of them.

"O'Malley, kiss me, please? I want to taste you again. I want to slip my hand beneath this gown and make you moan with need. A need that is as powerful and aching as the one I have for you."

He gently brushed his mouth over hers once and then again. He wanted to pull her closer, but worried about her wounds. But her mouth was not hurt and he planned to take as much as she would let him.

Moving his tongue along her lips, just at the opening of her mouth, he moaned at the heat he felt there. When she opened her mouth slightly and pulled his lower lip into her mouth, he moaned her name. "O'Malley, you're killing me, love."

He put his hand on her hip and pulled her closer without much effort. He deepened the kiss and swirled his tongue along hers and tasted her. He tasted her groan and gripped her tighter to him.

He cock was hard and straining at his zipper. He wanted her, wanted her with a passion he didn't think he had ever felt before. When her arms wrapped around his neck and she pulled him closer to her, he knew he was lost.

Spencer wanted to feel her beneath him, wanted to bury himself deep into her and lose himself in her. Gripping her other hip, he pushed his thigh between her legs and lifted her high on his body. Her legs wrapped around his hips and he pressed her back more against the wall; her body fit his perfectly.

"Christ, O'Malley, I want to be inside of you now." He rocked against her hard over and over.

"Please, Grant. Hurry."

Finding her panties beneath the open robe and hospital gown, he located the tiny string around her hips and pulled. The ripping noise was loud in the room. Moving his hand down behind her, along the curve of her ass, he ran his finger along the seam of her until he found her wet heat. Her mouth ripped from his as she threw back her head in a deep moan. When her hands started pulling at the snap of his pants, he knew that he was not going to make it. If she touched him, he knew he would come.

Stilling her hand with his, Spencer lifted the gown around her waist and found her clit, hard and wet. He slid his fingers into her from behind with his other hand. Her sheath gripped him, liquid and hot. She pulled at his fingers even as he ran his other hand lower into her tight curls.

"Come for me, O'Malley. Come for me and say my name." He found her clit again and pressed his thumb over it even as his other hand fucked her from behind. "Come, O'Malley."

She stiffened and he covered her mouth with his to capture her release. She pressed hard against his hand as she came, riding him over and over. Even with his mouth over hers, he could hear her scream. Her face, beautiful when she looked at him, was amazing when she climaxed. He pulled back to look at her as she continued to pulse around his fingers and his body.

When she looked up at him, her eyes were hooded and dazed-looking. She was lax in his arms; her legs now hung loose at his waist. He grinned down at her.

"Hi, you're beautiful, did you know that? I didn't hear my name, O'Malley. You promised you'd say it in the throes of passion."

"There was a tongue in my throat. And you cheated. Maybe next time we can get there together. If there is a next time."

"Oh, sweetheart, there will be a next time — lots of next times." He pressed hard into her and her moan made him realize how badly he wanted to come inside this woman, needed to be there. She responded by tightening her legs around him again and she rocked up against him. His cock ached to be released.

"Grant, if you don't have protection, this isn't going to happen. At least not like we both want. Undo your pants. I want to hold you, feel you in my hand. I really need to taste you. Can I feel your cock in my mouth, Grant?"

With her legs around him, he moved his hands to his pants and unsnapped them. Pulling down the zipper, his cock leapt out, a stream of pre-cum already dripping from the slit. Her hand wrapping around him made him jerk hard and more of his creamy liquid leaked from the tip.

"I'm so close, O'Malley. Too close for much more touching unless you want me to come all over you."

"I don't want you to come over me, but in me. I want to taste you, Grant. I want your cock in my mouth."

"Christ." She never let go of him as her legs slid down his legs. He was panting so hard that he was dizzy with it. He needed to either slow down or it was going to be difficult to explain how he had come to be half naked and unconscious on her floor. But within seconds, it didn't matter. Within seconds, he couldn't think of anything. As soon as her mouth closed over him, he couldn't have told anyone his name even if his life depended on it.

~~~

His cock was long and thick. Tasting his juices, she moaned deep in her throat, sending a vibration along his cock and making him moan again. He tasted so good; she knew that she was going to make him come even if she had work at it all night. But she didn't think she would need to.

Running her tongue along the heavy vein along his shaft, she followed it from the tip to the heavy sac at his groin, nipping gently as she went. She took one ball into her mouth and rolled it with her tongue then gave the other the same massage. When she made her way back up, she slid her hand up his thigh and gently fondled his balls, feeling them tighten and pull against his body. Wrapping her mouth over the purple, bulbous head, she moved her other hand up and down his shaft, using her saliva to make the ride smooth. His fingers wrapped around her head. He started to gently pump into her mouth.

"Baby. I'm going to...Christ, Caitlynne, I'm coming." His first hot jet of cum hit the back of her throat and she gagged slightly and nearly fainted from the taste of him. He was hot, lava hot, and spicy.

As more filled her mouth and throat, she started swallowing his offering as he pumped harder and faster into her. Reaching between her legs, she circled her wet slit and started fingering her clit as his body continued to fill her. When she felt her body responding to her fingers, she threw back her head and came hard even as his cock sprayed his last bit of cum over her face and mouth.

"Yes, oh yes, oh yes, oh yes!" She tried to be quiet; she had even thought that biting her lip would help. But it didn't; she loved coming with him.

He collapsed against the wall and panted above her. Her own breathing was not steady and she didn't think she could stand yet. Looking up at him from her position, she could see that his eyes were closed and there was a smile on his mouth.

"Are you all right?" she asked him. Cait was grinning too, and couldn't seem to stop looking up at him. He was the most beautiful man she had ever seen.

"No. No, I don't believe I will ever be all right again. Are you all right? Christ, O'Malley, you are in the hospital and here I am fucking you against the wall like some randy kid."

KATHI S. BARTON

He helped her up and lifted her gown to clean her face. When he was finished, he kissed her again. She felt her body begin to respond to him, his closeness, and his touch. When he picked her up and placed her gently on the bed without breaking the kiss, she knew she was in trouble. This couldn't happen. It wasn't safe, not safe for any of them.

"Grant, you know that we can't...that I'm going back to Chicago in a few days. You know that right?"

"Yeah, but until then I can try and persuade you to stay. Don't argue with me please. This was amazing and you're amazing. Just think about it, all right?"

"It was just sex. Great sex, but only sex. I can't stay here. I have a place, a job. I have to go back." She watched as his face hardened, seemed to freeze, as did her heart for saying this to him. But it was necessary; she couldn't hurt him. Couldn't put him into a position where he would be hurt like her family had been.

"Just sex, huh? I see. Well, thanks for clearing that up for me, O'Malley. I guess that's why you won't say my first name, not ever during just sex. Too personal for you, right? I'm glad to find out now, I guess, on just how you feel. I'm sorry for you. I'm going home and, don't worry, I won't be bothering you again." Without a backward glance or another word, he left even as he was tucking his shirt in.

She knew that she had hurt him. Hell, she hurt herself, but he was better off with it ending like this, much better than when he figured out that she was more horrible than he thought she was right now.

54

~Chapter Six~

"I see no reason why you shouldn't be able to go home in the morning, young lady. Keeping you here would be a waste of the good tax payers' money. I don't approve of all this extra detail with the police hanging about my halls when they could be doing something much more productive, like taking care of the blacks in this area."

"Yes, sir." Cait seethed. She didn't like this man and could not understand why someone hadn't shot him yet. He was a bigoted ass and his racial slurs where enough to make anyone want to hurt him.

Doctor Patterson had been in earlier, but as she was out in one of the visitors' lounges, Cait had not seen him. He had come by again this evening because he had been downstairs looking at some "nappy girl," and he thought he might try her again.

"Try to stay out of the line of fire when you go back to your job. I don't know why they let women out in the line of duty anyway. You people need to be put behind a desk, or better yet, stay at home where you belong."

Devin Grant walked in her room just as the good doctor finished his advice. Cait had had enough. She didn't know if it was because another ass of a man had walked in, or if she was just generally pissed off at all men, but she snapped.

"Doctor, if you don't leave my room this very second and take your bigoted, prejudice, small minded fucking ass out of here, I will not be responsible for what I do to you. You have done everything but put on a white robe and cape since you've been in here spouting your asinine opinions. I'm sick of it and do not have to listen to it for one more second. You are, by and far, the most...get the fuck out, now!" She knew that she look murderous; frankly, she didn't care.

"Why, young lady, no one speaks to me…"

"Get out!" She grabbed the pillow behind her and would have thrown it at him, but a sharp look at Devin and him shaking his head had her tossing it to the floor instead. She was boiling mad, something she hadn't been since she was a child.

The doctor left and Cait got up without a word and stormed to the bathroom. She hoped that her room would be empty when she came out. No such luck.

"Got any more threats for me today, Mr. Grant? If not, then you can get the hell out too. I've had enough of people today, thank you very much."

"I talked to Spence," he told her calmly. She didn't like the smile on his face; it looked too knowing to her. And she was positive that she didn't want to have this conversation with him either.

"Good for you. If that's all, then I want you to leave me alone. If you want help on your suicide, then tough. I'm going home tomorrow and I really want to rest up for the journey."

"You're going to be served in the morning. I just thought you'd like to know. I need you to stick around until the pre-trial of the teacher. I'd also like to use you as an expert witness in the murder of William, not suicide."

"No and hell no. I can't do a flipping thing about the pre-trial; that's a done deal. As for the other, fuck off."

He set his briefcase on the little table and opened it. He was taking his time for whatever he was looking for. And whatever it was, she knew that she was not going to give in.

"This is from my niece. She isn't allowed to come up and see you because she's only six. The others are from the other children in her class. We all know, their families, if it hadn't been for you, that it could have been a lot different of an outcome. Thank you."

She took the stack of cards. There were nine of them, brightly colored and covered in glitter and hunks of dried glue. The handwriting was uneven and her name had been spelt "cat." One child had even drawn a kitten on his for her. Ribbons and dollies decorated the inside of them, words of thanks and good wishes.

"You play dirty. I really hate you right now. I hope you know that. Why can't a man just be...go away, Mr. Grant."She wanted to toss the cards in the trash, but found that she couldn't.

"Good. That was my plan all along, for you to hate me. And if we're going to be working together, then

I'd like for you to call me Devin." She looked up at him and saw Spencer in this man's smile. Her heart clenched again. She looked down at the cards as she spoke to him. Maybe if...

"Mr. Grant, I'm not...I don't have it in me to be anything to your brother. You see, I'd always been a geeky kid, so when the opportunity came up for me to test out of school, I took it. The summer I turned eleven, I graduated from high school, and my father wasn't there. He was my world, you see. Then one day, he was gone. He had been a beat cop. Working the streets, he'd told me, was in his blood. When I was nine years old, my father was shot in the line of duty. It wasn't anything stupendous, or even all that noteworthy, at least to most. He had been killed by a kid who was handing him the gun his father had just killed his mother with. Dad had reached for it just as the little boy pulled the trigger and it got him in the heart."

"Oh, Caitlynne, I'm so sorry."

"My mother had never liked him being a cop, especially in a city as big as Chicago. She had told him that if he ever was killed, she wouldn't go to his funeral and would leave me to the world. She did too. The day after the men came to the house to tell us what had happened, she went into their room, filled the bath tub, climbed in, and slit her wrists. I found her. I knew then that I could never fall in love. Never marry, and never leave others behind as my parents had done to me. I can't hurt him, Mr. Grant. And I will. I love what I do, and I'm damned good at it. I'm sorry."

"You didn't tell him this, did you? You know my brother isn't as weak as your mother, nor is he stupid. He would understand what this means to you and support you. You need to tell him before he finds out from someone else."

"Are you threatening me? It doesn't matter. I know he's not weak, and I'm well aware of the fact that he isn't stupid. But what happens when I'm killed? Because we both know it's a good possibility. How could I do that do him?"

He pulled out a file and handed it to her. He picked up his briefcase and walked toward the door. "You'll never know, will you, if you don't tell him? The pre-trial is the day after tomorrow. I'll need you in the courthouse at seven o'clock. If you have any questions, call me. My number's in the file there. Goodnight, detective."

The nurse came in about twenty minutes after Devin left and gave her the paperwork she would need to leave. The nurse told her that the doctor told her if she could get a ride tonight, then he would appreciate it if Cait left his hospital, the sooner the better. She called her uncle Paddy.

After calling the department and telling them she had been released early and would no longer require the guard, she went to the bathroom to change. Her uncle arrived at midnight and with the help of the now off duty officer, she gathered up her things and left. A hospital administrator came in and talked to her about Patterson before she left as well. He seemed to think she was right about him, but did not come out and say so.

"Hungry, Caddy-did? Your aunt's been cooking up a storm since you called. She said that you needed to fatten up after all that hospital food. I got some of that chili left over, too, and there are a couple of subs in the icebox. I even picked up some of that tea you been drinking, that nasty unsweetened shit you drink by the gallon. I was supposed to pick up some ice cream too, but I didn't know what kind. I know you like chocolate, but they got about fifty kinds. What the hell happened to just plain old chocolate is what I want—"

"It's okay, Uncle Paddy. I'm fine. As soon as this is over, I'm going back to Chicago and you and Aunt Dee can come and visit me for a few weeks. Okay?"

"You can't keep doing this, darling. I'd miss you, and your Aunt D, she would be devastated if you were to go like your daddy. You have to stay safe. If not for me, then for her."

When they pulled into the drive, she reached over and hugged him. She loved this man more than he could ever know. He had been her solid foundation in a rocky life and she felt she would never be able to repay him.

She had no more than walked in the door tonight when Aunt Dee was making her a plate. The food was delicious, but she just wasn't all that hungry. After playing with her food for an hour and trying to stay cheery for her aunt and uncle, she begged off and went to her room.

She walked into the large bathroom and stood in front of the mirror for several minutes just staring at her face. She had to do this. She had to do it now or she would never be able to. Cait took off her shirt and stared at the bandages that covered most of her chest. Peeling back the tape under her right breast, she watched what she was doing and not what she was unveiling. After taking several deep breaths, she looked.

The wound was an angry red and the stitches were dark against her pale skin. The bruises were fading, but still a few days from being gone. Reaching up gently, she touched the skin around the area and winced at the fierce pain still there. Toby had shot her here first and she remembered the pain like it was happening again. She had to lean against the sink to fight the wave of dizziness. When she looked in the mirror again, she was crying and knew that she could not look at the other two now.

Pulling on her shirt again, she went to her room, sat on the big bed, and leaned back against the headboard. That's when she remembered the file. Reaching for it, she opened it and burst out laughing.

Inside were pictures of what she assumed was Spencer growing up. He had been as much a geek as she had been. She looked through them one at a time, then spread them out all over the bed and looked at the man he had become. There were also pictures of him and who she assumed were his brothers, and quite a few of him and his little girl. There were a few with an older couple and some with the woman and another man. Devin was a sly man and she was going to kill him the next time she saw him. This really was playing dirty.

She picked up the one with him and Meggie. It had been taken recently. She could tell because Meggie had not changed that much. They were both looking at the camera and smiling; they looked happy. So very happy. She put all the other pictures away and set the one of the two of them near her bed and lay down. She was asleep within minutes.

~~~

Spencer paced his bedroom. He was so angry that he wanted to hit something or someone. Not really, he realized, but he did need to get rid of some of this somewhere. Pacing his room helped.

Damn it, it was not just about sex. It was...okay, it was sex, but it had been incredible sex. Pacing, so lost in thought he almost missed his phone ringing. He pulled it out and grimaced when he saw who it was.

"I just spoke with your girlfriend. Damn but she's stubborn. We may not be best buds, but she likes me more than you right now," Devin teased him. Too bad he was not in the mood to enjoy it.

"Devin, I swear if you don't behave, poor Ronnie will be a widow very soon. And she'll have to raise that baby all by herself. Not that that's not a bad idea, but I will murder you."

Devin had been married less than six months and his pretty little bride and law partner was due in four months. Everyone was thrilled about it and the new baby, especially their mom.

"Ronnie said the same thing. By the way, she said to call her. Some nonsense about giving you advice about women. Anyway, court is set for eight o'clock day after tomorrow. I'm suggesting all the parents of the kids be there with their children. We'll let the judge see how serious we are about this. Can you and Meggie be there?"

Spencer was taking a light quarter this spring and then taking the summer off to be with Meggie. They were taking a vacation together, their first. But he would be there even if he had to cancel classes for the whole day.

"Yeah. Is O'Malley going to help you? Willingly help you, that is?" He hoped she would not just to piss off Devin, but knew that her testimony would help a great deal.

"No, not willingly, but she'll help. She got her badge back; she should be notified about it in the morning. A friend of mine called me tonight to let me know. Spence, did you know that she has a Gold Shield — pretty impressive for someone as young as she is. Internal affairs cleared her, but the trial is still on. I'll explain this weekend at Mom's. You bringing her along with you?"

"I'll ask her. O'Malley carries a gun; you think Mom will have a problem with that?" Their mom carried one in her car and sometimes in her purse. Being a parole officer could put her into some dicey situations. But O'Malley carried one all the time and he wondered how everyone would feel about that, especially Morgan, Nicky's wife.

"I wouldn't think so, but I would probably ask first. She wants to be called O'Malley then? I've never seen a person more determined to call someone by their last name like she does. Why do you think that is?"

"Yes. She calls me Grant, so it works for us. I think it might have something to do with working in the atmosphere that she does." She was going to call him Grant at least until they were in bed together. Which reminded him, he had to pick up protection. Even though she was mad at him, it didn't keep him from wanting her.

Spencer went to Meggie's room to check on her after he hung up with Devin. He marveled that she was all his. She was going to be staying with him forever now and he had never been so happy.

Her mother, Shannon, had not even put up much of a fight. She had just demanded that he pay her a lump sum of cash and then be done with it. Devin had drawn up the contract for them and even though he did not like the way Shannon had coldly done it, he was glad it was over too. It had been a long, five year battle.

Looking around her room, he grimaced. Boxes of stuff were everywhere and her windows still only had shades on them. He had wanted to have it decorated before they moved in, but his mom had told him to wait and let Meggie decide. He looked over at the books of wallpaper samples the previous decorator had left and smiled. The woman, Desire, had left in a major huff two days ago when Meggie refused to let her do it her way. Desire had thought that she could get into Daddy's pants too. Not going to happen.

Spencer wondered what O'Malley would do to the room. He thought of her and Meggie bent over swatches and laughed out loud. Nope, he thought, he could only see them bending over O'Malley's gun and her showing Meggie how it worked and how to be safe around it. Meggie would be a willing pupil too.

Smiling, he left his daughter with a light kiss to her forehead and went to his own room.

~CHAPTER SEVEN~

Cait was at the court house at seven-thirty. She was never late for work and found no reason to be late for this either. She hated court appearances; it was not so much the court itself, but having to dress in nicer clothes. She looked down at the clothes she had on.

She had lost weight. Not a lot, but enough that her clothes hung on her tall frame. Her pants were dark blue and light cotton; they looked good only because her aunt Dee had ironed them for her. Her shoes were her service shoes, but it was all she had with her, and she was not spending money on shoes she would wear the one time. She had put on a silk blouse her aunt had lent her because it was so hot out for this time of year, and a dark jacket over that. Her service weapon, another Glock, but a twenty-two this time, was in a shoulder holster under her right arm and there were two clips in the harness strap. She also had another Glock, a twenty-seven this time, strapped to her ankle. It, too, had two extra clips strapped to her other ankle.

The clips were interchangeable and most cops she knew carried the same combination of weapons for that reason. She was glad for their weight and comfort again. Her badge was on a chain around her neck and was currently tucked into her inside jacket pocket. There was also a pair of steel handcuffs, OC spray, and a couple of knives tucked here and there on her body.

When Devin Grant approached her, she saw him hesitate slightly then move forward. Cait was used to that. Most men, even very strong men like the Grant men, were intimated by her status and the fact that she carried a gun. She could live with that.

"I think you looked less scary in the hospital holding a gun on Spencer than you do now. I never realized that how a person dresses—especially you—could convey so much authority and respect. You wear your job well, Detective."

"How's the murder going? You know that it's more than likely someone close to him, probably the wife." She didn't know what to say to the statement about her clothing and chose to ignore it for now.

"The wife made a full confession late last night based on your information. Thank you. She said that William was asking for a divorce and since she had signed a pre-nup, she would get nothing more than what she went into the marriage with. She said she wanted her fair share and since she was the guilty party, and she wouldn't get squat. She was having an affair with William's seventeen-year-old son. We're still trying to find him."

Cait nodded. Nerves made her pace and she had been pacing a lot this morning. Between the pacing and worrying with the necklace around her throat, she was a bundle of nerves. She was glad for the distraction of the case to think about. Her mind rarely shut down and it didn't now either.

"You do know that the kid is either dead or she has him stashed somewhere? He wouldn't have been in on it though. He's probably in Venezuela if there is a house there that William owned. I would check there first."

"Okay, I will. Why Venezuela? Not that I don't believe you, but why that particular place, I guess?" He had pulled out a pad of paper from his jacket pocket and was making notes. She didn't know why, but she found she liked that. But she was still pissed at him, so kept the compliment to herself.

"There was a paperweight on the desk and several pictures that had references on and in them. The paperweight was something small. Those sorts of things are what you remember, but not the details of why. She would have seen them there and it would have been in the forefront of her mind when she was planning her move."

The bailiff came out to tell them they were next and Devin led Cait inside. She was just being seated when a lovely woman sat down next to her and smiled.

"Hello. You must be Spencer's detective. My, you are as beautiful as he said. I'm Ronnie Grant, by the way, Devin's wife. Sorry I'm late. Morning sickness is hell."

Cait nodded. She was not sure she liked to be referred to as Spencer's anything, but said nothing. A minute later, Spencer walked in with a group of people and Meggie. Her breath caught in her throat.

He was dressed in a suit this time, but it was pressed and neat. His hair was combed, but still looked mussy, like he had just been tumbled by a woman. He had on dark glasses and when Meggie pulled them off for him and tucked them into his pocket, he smiled and Cait's body clenched. Christ, she thought, a smile like that could hurt a girl if it was directed at her.

Cait turned around and noticed that Ronnie was smiling at her. Cait flushed at the knowing grin.

"They can make your panties wet when they do that, can't they? Sorry. I got pregnant and I can't seem to control my mouth anymore."

Cait thought she was right. In both the panties and her mouth observation, but again, didn't say anything. She turned back to the front and tried to ignore the man and the child behind her. It was not as easy as it sounded.

The judge came in before Ronnie could say anything else and Counselor Clamp, the teacher's attorney, called Ms. Ames to the stand.

~~~

Spencer tried to listen to what was going on, but all he could think about was the woman seated two rows in front of him. When she had turned around and looked at him, he could see the desire flare in her face and eyes, and he nearly leapt over the seats to get to her. He wondered what Ronnie had said to her to make her blush and decided to take Ronnie up on her offer of advice.

Meggie tugging on him brought him from his wonderings. Good thing, too; his cock was hurting again and this was no time to have a hard-on.

"Can I go up with Aunt Ronnie and Mal?" she was asking him. He started to say no, but if he could convince O'Malley to see him, then he needed to see how she reacted to his daughter, and nodded for her to go.

Spencer thought she would just go up and sit on the empty chair next to O'Malley, but Meggie, never one to be shy, crawled up into O'Malley's lap. He could not see either face, but Ronnie turned and winked at him and he felt himself relax somewhat. Yeah, he was going to talk to Ronnie.

Spencer was just becoming really bored when O'Malley stood with Meggie and came back to him. Concern was all over her face. He looked around the courtroom to see what might be her worry, but saw nothing.

"Take her out. Don't let her speak anymore until I come out to explain." Her whisper was urgent. Spencer didn't hesitate, but took Meggie out into the hall. Paddy O'Malley followed.

"What's happening?" Spencer asked the older O'Malley. Meggie had sat quietly on the bench when he had asked her to.

"Doona know, but she gave me the signal and I hightailed it out here too. She's got something up her sleeve, you can bet that." Spence noted that Dee had come out and was sitting next to Meggie.

Spencer watched as his daughter walked over and went right into Paddy's arms and started talking to him. The man spoke back and before Spencer could wonder about it; both Cait and Ronnie came out arguing.

"I said to squeak, not make the man think you were in labor, for cripes sake. You scared the shit out of him," Cait was saying as she hurried out the door of the session.

"I do not squeak. And it got him back to you, didn't it? I think it was a brilliant plan and I think we'll use it again sometime. Hello, Spencer. I love your girlfriend," Ronnie said as she hugged him. Cait walked over to her uncle and was talking to him when Meggie came back to him. He couldn't hear what they were saying, but Paddy was nodding and smiling a lot.

"What's going on? She told me to take Meggie out and she would explain and her uncle doesn't know either."

"Oh, I've got to learn sign language faster. I'm not sure; it was something Meggie said to Cait. She whispered it to Devin when he came back to see if I was in labor. You should have seen his face. It was priceless." Ronnie laughed.

"It was not priceless; it was mean. You were just supposed to...never mind. Thanks for your help. But if he beats your butt like he said he was going to, then don't come running to me. I need to speak to Grant; can you please keep an eye on Meggie for a moment?"

When Ronnie and Meggie walked away together, Cait stepped up to him and took a deep breath. When she closed her eyes and leaned to him, he nearly reached out to pull her into his arms. His cock hardened more.

"You smell too good to be allow out in public. You should be considered lethal and put in a bubble. Listen, Meggie told me that Ms. Ames has brown bottles in her desk and that she drinks them all day long. I didn't ask her if it was beer because I wasn't sure she would know what it was. Does she, you think?"

"Not that I'm aware of. I mean, I've had one at Mom's or out with my brothers, but there isn't any in our house. But until recently, she was living with her mother, so maybe. Why, is that important?"

"Just for future reference, Grant, don't kiss me with beer on your breath. I don't like it and I hate the taste. Uncle Paddy is going to call a favor in and have the police go to the school and check out Ms. Ames' desk. If there is beer there, that's a class A felon and the rest of this is just gravy. If not, then we aren't out anything but some time."

"Am I going to get to kiss you again, O'Malley — taste you?" He heard the rest, but all he could focus on was her mouth and the tingling sensation of knowing he was going to get to taste her again.

"If you play your cards right. Are you listening to me, Grant? I said—"

He gave in and he kissed her. Her mouth was closed when he first touched his mouth to hers and he may have stopped with just a small kiss, but when she groaned and opened under him, he pulled her closer and deepened it.

Hot and wet and she tasted of cinnamon and sugar. Need and desire moved through him and he rocked into her gently. When her arms came up and over his shoulders, he tightened his arms around her waist and moaned. Her tongue swirled against his and she suckled it into her mouth. Spencer could feel his blood heating and everything going on around them simply faded out.

"You two wanna come up for air? I doona think this is the place for what you're currently doing to each other. I'm pretty sure that it's illegal in all fifty states."

"Go away, Uncle Paddy. I'm busy," Cait said to her uncle, then she went back to kissing him. Spencer didn't mind.

He heard the man chuckle as Cait pulled away slightly. He didn't let her go because he wasn't sure he could stand if he didn't have her support.

"The police are going to the school now. It's an anonymous tip; dinna think you wanted it bandied about that the information came from a six-year-old," Paddy said.

"Good. Thanks, Mr. O'Malley. I appreciate your discretion on this. You're right about my daughter." He looked over at the man and noticed an odd look on his face. Spencer was about to ask when Paddy laughed at him.

"Boy, you play tonsil tag with my Caddy-did like that, you can damn well call me Paddy, don't you think?"

Spencer flushed, but was saved from further embarrassment by the bailiff calling Cait to the courtroom.

~Chapter Eight~

"Do you swear to tell the whole truth and nothing but the truth, so help you God?" The bailiff was smiling at her. She knew he had seen her kissing Grant in the hall. It didn't embarrass her so much as made her want more. Spencer was fast becoming addictive.

"I do."

"Please state your full name and your occupation for the clerk, please."

"Caitlynne Alexander O'Malley, detective third grade, homicide, Chicago PD. I'm also carrying and I have my badge." The bailiff nodded. Cait had filed a request when she came in, so he had probably been made aware of it.

"Homicide? I didn't hear anyone was killed. Why didn't someone tell me that the venue had changed?" Judge demanded of his bailiff.

"No, Your Honor, I'm here as a witness for the prosecution. Not as a detective. I apologize for the misunderstanding," Cait quickly explained.

"You related to that old Irishman O'Malley that was in here earlier this morning, Detective?"

"Yes, sir. He's my uncle, Patrick O'Malley. He's running an errand for me, sir. He'll be back soon."

"He's a good man. You come from good stock. Let's get this show started. Counselor, start."

"Miss O'Malley, it says here you are on administrative leave; is that true?" Phillip Clamp asked her.

"It's Detective, and no."

"You're not on leave? I thought the file said that you were...let me find it. Yes, you're on leave until your doctor releases you."

"Yes."

He looked up at her, confusion written all over his face. Cait just stared back at him. She had learned from enough court appearances that you never volunteered information to a lawyer, not even your own. Ever.

"Yes, you're on administrative leave?"

"No," she answered. Now it was just plain fun. Messing with an attorney, any attorney, was a point in her favor, she thought.

"Miss O'Malley, you need to be —"

"It's Detective O'Malley. I would very much appreciate if you would remember that, Counselor. I worked very hard for that title." She knew she should not have snapped, but she was getting aggravated, as well, at his refusal to acknowledge her status.

"Your Honor, Detective O'Malley is being very uncooperative. Is there anything you can do to help me with this?"

Cait snorted, but didn't open her mouth.

"Detective, could you please tell the counselor what he wants to know? He seems to be under the misunderstanding that you are supposed to read his mind."

"No, I'm not on administrative leave. Yes, I'm on leave."

"So, you are on leave. I guess I don't understand what the issue is." He looked at her expectantly and she looked back. "Detective?"

"Yes?"

"I asked you a question. The judge has instructed you to answer my questions, remember?" He had a tone. Not even a little one either.

Cait looked at Devin and then at the judge. She didn't hear a question and, apparently, neither of them had either.

"You asked me if I remember the instructions, which I do. Prior to that, you whined...sorry, asked the judge to make me answer you. But other than that, you've not asked me anything. Usually, at least the last I heard, a question is started with a 'who, what, when, where'...you get the idea. You stated a fact, not asked a question. You want me to answer something?"

"Are you trying to be smart?" He was snarling now. It didn't bother her, but she did refrain from laughing — out loud anyway.

"One of us should to be."

"Your Honor..." The courtroom was having the worst case of sudden coughing in history, Cait thought. Even the judge was having a hard time keeping a straight face. Cait looked at Spencer and he winked at her.

"Counselor, perhaps you need to pretend you're on that show where you have to answer things in the form of a question. Could help you with the detective, I'm thinking," the judge informed him. Cait was sure there was another small tone there, but then, she didn't know the judge all that well.

"What sort of leave are you on?" All pretense of politeness was gone.

Finally, she thought.

"Medical."

"Was that so hard? What is the difference between the administrative leave and the medical leave you are currently on?"

"Medical means someone has been bad to me; administrative means I've been bad to someone else. And before you ask, yes, I've been bad before. Very bad."

"Your Honor, while this is very educating, do you think we could maybe move on to the case at hand now that Mr. Clamp has a handle on how to ask questions?" Devin asked as he stood. Cait noticed that he, too, was having a hard time not laughing at the other lawyer.

"Move on, Counselor."

"Detective O'Malley, can you tell us why in your report to the police you suggested that Ms. Ames should be charged with attempted homicide?"

"Yes."

Cait could swear she could see the steam roll out of his ears and she had to look down at her hands before she could look up at him again. At this point, she thought he might strangle her without much thought to the consequences.

"Detective O'Malley, tell us why you think Ms. Ames should be charged with attempted homicide," Clamp said to her.

"The minors were tethered to the post with no means of escape. They were also without visual adult supervision."

"Escape? Wouldn't that be what the tether, as you called it, would have been for, keeping them together and safe? I can understand you being concerned about the children and them without adult supervision, but that still doesn't mean homicide. Please, tell us in your opinion why you would come to such a conclusion."

"You have a child under the age of one who is having issues with its formula, correct?" She hated to play this way, but he had asked her opinion.

The lawyer looked at the judge then back at her. His face registered first disbelief then anger.

"How did you...?"

"I wouldn't be much of a homicide detective if I didn't notice things. There is formula on your shoulder and you smell of baby powder and lanoline. I would guess you changed a diaper before leaving for work and you cuddled a kid. Diapers tell me it's yours; otherwise, you'd have left that job to the parents. You have no shine on your otherwise shiny shoes; that indicates that you lack time very recently. You either have a new sick baby or you have very weird eating habits, as well as bathing ones."

"A baby. He's five weeks old. But what does that have to do — "

"Imagine, if you can, those nine children tied to that pole, and little Bobby Clamp is one of them. The driver comes barreling down the street and slams on his brakes. He nose dives his car to stop — this time. Yes, he was speeding; posted limit in that area is thirty-five, but he was traveling at about forty-two easy. That aside, because going thirty-five or fifty-five, had he have swerved instead of braking there, would have been a fifty-fifty chance he would have driven into those children. They had no means of escape, no one to pull them to safety, and not one of them could hear the shouts of the others around them. At either speed, all nine, plus little Bobby, would be dead. How would you feel about that? How would you have felt knowing that the teacher, the one you have entrusted to keep them safe from the hours of eight until three, took them to the store, and tied them to a pole so that she could go into a store and purchase a beer?"

The room was quiet. Counselor Clamp had to lean back against his table, his face pale and drawn. Cait looked over at Devin and he, too, was pale. She was beginning to think she had gone too far when the back doors to the court room opened and three uniformed officers and a nicely dressed detective walked in. Cait's uncle was right behind them.

"Sorry for the interruption, Your Honor, but we have an arrest warrant for Miss Amelia Ames on child endangerment, reckless endangerment, delinquency of a minor, public intoxication."

"That's a lie!" Ms. Ames jumped up. "I never once offered them damned brats any of my beer."

Cait couldn't help it. All the stress of the past few weeks, she just burst out laughing.

~~~

Spencer watched as O'Malley talked with the police who had arrested Ms. Ames. She looked so at ease and happy. His family had gone to lunch and he was to bring her along with him. Paddy O'Malley clapped him on his shoulder as he came up behind Spencer.

"Got it bad, don't you, laddie?"

Spencer didn't answer, but smiled at the man. But yeah, he had it bad.

"She's all I got left of my brother. She's a good girl, but it will take a hell of a man to claim her."

"She and I just met, Paddy. I'm not sure either of us is ready to talk about claiming each other. Besides, she's made it perfectly clear that she's leaving as soon as this is over."

"Maybe. That brother of yours, the one that's a lawyer, he's been using her for another case, ain't he?"

"I think so. But he pissed her off and she told him she wouldn't help him anymore. She has a hell of a stubborn way about her, he said."

He looked down at the little man and noticed a twinkle in his eye. Spencer smiled; he thought it suited the man, for some reason.

"He'd be correct in that—got that from my sister, Dee. She was two weeks late, wouldn't be born until she was ready. Same way with my Caddy-did."

Spencer had thought that Dee was Paddy's wife and was surprised to hear otherwise. He looked over at the woman in question and noticed that she seemed to know as many of the police as Paddy did.

Cait shook hands with Captain Tucker and then she was walking toward him. He barely registered

Paddy's comment about having it really bad. Watching her and not tackling her to the floor to kiss her took every ounce of his concentration.

"That went well, don't you think?" she asked him, and then frowned. The smile she had slowly slipped from her lovely face.

"My family is going to celebrate and you and your family are to come too. My mom said to tell you that you'd better be there; she would hate to have to kick your butt." Spencer moved a curl from her cheek and ran his fingers down her shoulder to her hand.

"Okay. Are you all right, Grant? You look...I don't know. Did I do something to upset you? If this is about me and Meggie, I just didn't want her to warn the teacher."

"No, nothing like that. I want you, O'Malley. I've never wanted a woman as much as I want you. Right now, against the wall, on the floor, standing here with you wrapped around me. I want you hard; I want you fast. I want you now."

"Oh my." Her voice was breathy. And her eyes had become darker; her pulse at her throat was pounding. Spencer found he wanted to sink his teeth into her there and taste her.

He reached out to pull her to him, but her uncle Paddy came up behind him again and it was everything Spencer could do not to snarl at the man.

"Come on, you two, before you're arrested. You have to ride with me and Dee. Your family has already left." With a quick kiss, Cait pulled away, but held his hand as they walked to the car.

~CHAPTER NINE~

Cait was used to loud rooms. The squad room sometimes sounded like a locker room and a football stadium at the same time with phones ringing, loud shouts of anger, and humor. But this was entirely different. These were families.

They had been shown a private room when they entered the restaurant. Everyone they met, the staff and owners, seemed to know the Grants. Even her uncle was not a stranger to some of the women they saw.

There was a long table set up in the middle of the huge room. It was blessedly cool and Cait took a deep breath as soon as she walked in.

Meggie rushed to her dad and he scooped her up into his arms. Meggie gave her daddy a big kiss and then starting telling him about the ride over and also how she loved talking to Cait's aunt Dee.

Cait's aunt had been born deaf. A product of a severe infection that her mother had had in the later months of pregnancy, Cait had been told as a child. Dee had come to the United States from Ireland to help her brother Paddy raise Cait when she became an orphan after the death of her parents.

"She wants to know if she can sit next to you during lunch. You don't have to, O'Malley; my mom will be happy to let her sit with her," Spencer said.

"No, that'll be great. Just no checkers." Cait signed to Meggie her answer and smiled when Meggie gave her a huge kiss as well.

"Spencer, bring the girl of the hour over to meet the rest of your family, please. I'm sure she needs to sit down and take a break. You can suck face with her later." Cait glared at the man, who just laughed at her.

"Behave, Byron. We happen to like sucking face, thank you. You should meet my family," Spencer told her. "Let me introduce you. Everyone, this is Caitlynne O'Malley. She's a detective from Chicago. This is her uncle, Paddy O'Malley, a retired detective, and her aunt Dee, Paddy's sister."

Everyone stood and said their name. Cait knew a couple of them already, but most of them were strangers. She had not realized that Spencer had so many brothers, but immediately could tell that they were related to each other.

Ordering became the first order of business and the waitress brought in several pitchers of beer and mugs. Cait let hers sit empty in front of her. She didn't like alcohol and detested the smell and taste of beer. Her attention was on what Meggie was saying to her when she heard Spencer being teased about not having a brew with his brothers.

"Sorry, guys, but some people don't enjoy beer breath and since I plan on partaking of some of her later, I'll pass."

Cait, used to male banter and who had no problem taking care of herself in a dirty joke, turned to Spencer. "You planning to get lucky later, teach? 'Cause if you think not having beer breath will help you, you have another thing coming."

When he reached over, pulled her to him, and kissed her full on the lips, she nearly squeaked out loud. Then when he slid his tongue along her lips, she melted against him. The room just faded away at the feeling of him and his mouth.

When he pulled away, she actually whimpered and then flushed when she realized that everyone close to them heard her. She was more embarrassed that he had kissed her in front of his family than she was about her reaction.

"Oh yeah, O'Malley, I plan to get very lucky later. And so will you. Over and over and over again," he whispered in her ear.

Plates were being served around the table when Paddy turned to Ronnie. They had been talking since the older man sat next to her. Cait smiled at her uncle; he was the biggest flirt she knew.

"Hey, girly, what was with that loud squeak you made in the courtroom? Nearly had me a heart attack when you did it. Then that husband of yours leaping over the desk at you. I was afreared he'd have himself a babe right there."

"She made me do it," Ronnie exclaimed, pointing at Cait.

"Me? I asked you, very quietly I might add, to get your husband's attention so that he could come back to us without raising a ruckus. How the hel...heck was I supposed to know you were going to make a noise like a rhino giving birth? A simple clearing of the throat might have done it, you know."

"I most certainly did not make any sort of noise like that. I merely made a small noise in the back of my throat to get his attention. You did say it was important. I wanted to help," Ronnie said as she glanced at her husband.

"Oh you helped all right, Mrs. Grant. He leapt over that railing like he was going to murder me or deliver your kid. The man looked pole axed when I asked him to stall and what we had discovered. I had to repeat myself four times before he understood that I was not hurting you."

"It's Ronnie, and he did look very sexy, didn't he? He was all scary and protective. Don't you just love a manly man?"

Cait rolled her eyes at the woman. If pregnancy made a person this stupid, she was glad she never planned to have a kid. Devin kissed his wife and they all settled into their lunch.

About halfway through their meal, Meggie started to drift to the side. She tried to fight it and Cait thought she looked so adorable, but it was clear that she was going to fall off her chair if she continued listing. Cait simply picked her up and settled Meggie across her lap without pausing in her eating. Cait looked up and caught Mrs. Parker, Spencer's mom, staring at her with an odd look. Before she could ask her about it, Morgan asked about their Memorial Day plans that weekend.

"The caterer will be at the house on Friday afternoon to start setting up," Mrs. Parker told Morgan. "The hog will arrive then and so will the backhoe to dig the pit. The other food will come early Saturday morning. I hope things go as well as last year. That was so much fun."

Cait was only about half paying attention because Spencer was running his fingers up and down her arm gently. The room grew very warm and she started to slide her jacket off when a sharp intake of breath from Morgan stopped her. Cait realized her gun had been exposed to those at the table.

"I'm sorry. I never thought about it. Being around this is as much a part of me that your bag is to you. I never meant to startle you or frighten you." She was putting her jacket back on when Morgan spoke up.

"No, please don't. You're right. It is a part of you and if you're going to be hanging around us for a while, then I need to get used to it. I've just had some bad experiences with guns and I just never thought...I'm sorry, Cait." Morgan smiled and picked up her bag. "How did you know about the bag? I mean, you're right, but how did you know?"

"I'm paid to pay attention. You ever fire a gun, Mrs. Grant? I mean one that wasn't pointed at someone who was trying to hurt you?"

"How did...no, never. I've thought about it, but I've never gotten around to it. And I don't want one in the house with the boys."

"You can always be afraid of guns, but to respect them, you have to know them. They are only as dangerous as the person who thinks they know what they are doing. May I show you something?"

When Morgan nodded, Cait reached under her arm and pushed the small tab that released the magazine. She took it out and slipped it into her jacket pocket. Her uncle got up and sat in Meggie's chair and watched Cait's hands.

"Uncle Paddy is going to be my spotter. He'll make sure that the gun is not loaded, all right?" Cait released the gun from the holster and slid it out. With quick fingers, she slid the slide forward and the round ejected into the air. Cait caught it with one hand and slipped it, too, into her pocket, then handed the weapon to her uncle. "He'll check the chamber and the butt to make sure there are no rounds left in the weapon. But you should always assume that the gun is loaded even though you've seen us empty it."

Uncle Paddy handed the gun back to Cait, muzzle down. Once she slid the slide forward, he went back to his seat.

"This is a Glock twenty-two and as you can see, it's empty. This is a service weapon that most cops and detectives carry on the outside. This particular one was my father's backup weapon. Here, hold it in your hand and feel the weight. But be careful. Like I said, you always want to assume that it's loaded."

Morgan took the gun from her. Cait was impressed to see that she kept the barrel down at all times and did not shake it about the room. Glancing around, she noticed that they had an audience and that the room had gotten quiet.

"It doesn't weigh as much as I thought it would." And she handed it back to her. Cait took out the three clips and handed those to her.

"One of those would be in the weapon and at least two extra ones would be close enough for you to get to them. Most people on the force carry a second weapon and two clips for it as well." Cait, a long time cop, slipped a fresh clip back into the butt of the Glock and then racked on into the chamber. Without looking, she put the gun back into her shoulder holster and clipped the holster safety over the guard. She took out the single bullet and put it back into the clip, then put them back into her pocket.

"Do you carry a spare? I have a smaller one on my ankle most of the time and Devin bought me OC spray when we got married. I've never used the spray, but have pulled the gun a couple of times." When Ronnie looked over at her husband and he flushed, Cait laughed.

"OC is dangerous, Mrs. Grant, unless you know how to use it. Do you carry your concealed permit with you? It needs to be on your person at all times."

"Ronnie, and it's in my purse in the car. I didn't wear it today because we were going into the courthouse. I know they have a rule about carrying one inside the building. Come to think of it, how did you...a cop can carry inside, right? I guess I knew that but never thought about it." Ronnie nodded as she answered her own question. These people were an impressive lot.

89

KATHI S. BARTON

"Yes. I can carry mine into anywhere, but have to have my ID, too. If a cop pulls you over, he could take your weapon and arrest you. Your licenses need to be with you at all times. I'll get you a special holder that will hold both."

"You said that was your father's weapon. Where is he?"

Cait glared at Devin. He knew what had happened to her father; she had told him herself. "Dead. He was killed in the line of duty when I was Meggie's age and before you ask; my mother committed suicide two days later rather than face life with me at her side. Life is a bitch for a cop. It's been a lovely lunch, but I have to...I need to go. Thank you all very much."

Cait stood and scooped the little girl into her father's arms without waking her. Shoved would have been more accurate, but the need to escape was eminent. She needed air, right now.

Stumbling out, she heard Spencer say something, but she was having some difficulty breathing and it was making her slightly dizzy. Suddenly, arms were around her waist and after a brisk, "Come with me," she was out into the fresh air.

~CHAPTER TEN~

Spencer was going to kill his brother Devin. Right after he got O'Malley breathing again. When she stood up to leave, he thought is heart would stop. The thoughts that had run through his head had frightened him.

She had scared him when she started to leave. First, because he thought she was leaving for good, then because she had looked so pale. After giving Meggie to his mom, he ran after Cait and got her outside and to the car before she fainted. She was sitting on the trunk of Paddy's car, her head between her legs. She looked up at him, a watery smile on her face.

"I really hate your brother right now. He knew what happened to my dad. I think I'll kick him in the nuts next time I see him."

"Okay, sounds like a plan. I don't like him much right now either. Are you okay, honey?" Spencer leaned forward and pulled her into his arms. She felt so good there; he never wanted to let her go.

"Yes, I'm sorry. I ruined your lunch with—"

He silenced her with his mouth. He wondered how much longer he would be able to use this particular trick when her tongue suddenly moved along his lips. Then need for her swelled in his blood and nothing else mattered.

He knew they were in a public place, but he slid his legs between hers anyway, pulling her close to the edge of the car she was still sitting on. He knew that at any moment, someone would see what they were doing, but his need for her overrode all saneness. For as much as he wanted to throw her on the trunk and bury himself deep into her, he knew this was not the time or the place to do it.

"Let's go. My house is only ten minutes from here and I can get us there in five. Please, I want you, and without taking the chance of ending up in jail for indecent exposure, you need to come with me."

She giggled and his heart leapt. Christ, he thought. He did not just have it bad for her; he was terminal for her. He had never wanted anyone as much as he did her.

"You don't have a car and mine is at the courthouse. How do you expect to get us anywhere? Unless you can get a taxi to come here, I think we're stuck."

Spencer pulled out his key ring and found the one he was looking for. Serves Devin right, he thought as he walked over to his new SUV and opened it up. Smiling to her, he waved her over.

"Nice trick. Whose is this and won't they miss it when they come out after lunch? I'm pretty sure you and I didn't come here in this." She stood in front of him and kissed his nose.

"It's Devin's," he told her with a grin. She smiled too and got in the passenger side. As Spencer got into the driver's seat, he continued. "I'll drop you off at the lot to get your car. You can follow me to my house. He can pick up his car from my house."

"Okay. Are you planning to tell him at some point? He may deserve this and I'm all for making his life a little hell, but he might call the police. And all the same to you, I think shooting him would be easier than trying to explain why we stole his car."

"I'll let him know when we get on the road. Listen, O'Malley, I'm sorry about him upsetting you. I'll beat him to a bloody pulp when I see him next time."

"No. He was just forcing my hand. I...I had already told him what happened to my parents a week ago. I...I was trying to explain why I can't see you, why I can't get close to you."

Spencer thought about them getting more than close very soon, but decided that was not what she meant. She was not leaving him, not if he could help it. There was something here beginning between them and he wanted to see where it was going.

"Then explain it to me. Because, O'Malley, I really want to get close to you, very close. I like being around you and want to spend time getting to know you better," he demanded.

"You just want to get into my pants. That's fine with me. I want to get into yours as well. Your cock is all I've thought of for...what are you doing?"

Pulling over seemed a smart idea at that moment, as all the blood in his body had pooled in his groin. Tugging her closer so he could kiss her also seemed like a good idea until he realized that bucket seats were not conducive to the kind of kiss he had in mind. Pulling back a little, he saw that her eyes were glazed with need and darkened with desire.

"I have to call my brother and then I need to get you to your car. But if we don't leave right now, I'm going to drag you over to the nearest wall or tree and fuck you until neither of us can stand."

She was nodding and panting, driving him closer to the edge. He could see her nipples poking hard against the silk of her blouse and before he could stop himself, he flicked his finger over the stiffened peak. Her moan was deep and loud in the car.

"Hurry, Grant, or I'm going to come right now with or without you. You have my body on fire and if I get any wetter, the seat will need to be replaced. I want you inside of me now."

Turning around to the steering wheel again, he gripped it tight. Key, turn, shift and drive—following those simple words seemed to help and it got them moving again. He hoped nothing happened before he got her to her car, like stopping, or worse, someone asked him a question. He wasn't sure he had enough blood in his brain to make a coherent answer.

He dropped her off at the courthouse three minutes later. He would swear it was hours, but it just felt that way. Once she was in her car and it started, he pulled out his phone to call Devin.

"I have your car. And you may or may not get it back in one piece. What the fuck is wrong with you?" Spencer demanded of his brother as soon as Devin answered.

"Spencer, I'm so sorry. I was only trying to help you both out. She told me why she won't get serious with you and I thought she would open up. Please don't hurt my car; Ronnie is already pissed at me. I think Cait's uncle might have called in a few favors and I might be looking at some serious tickets in my near future."

"It would serve you right. I'd like to work things out with her on my own, thanks. Shit, Devin, did you see her face? She looked like you had killed her dad yourself. Don't you remember how it was when our dad was killed, how we felt?"

"Yes. I'm truly sorry. If it makes you feel any better, Mom is pissed at me too. And I may never get laid again." Spencer groaned. Now was not the time to discuss anyone's sex life.

"A little better. Tell Mom I'll come and get Meggie later tonight. O'Malley and I have some things to discuss." Spencer didn't know how much actual talking they would be doing, but it was better than telling his brother he was hoping to get laid himself.

"Talking, huh? I'm sure you do. If Mom can't take Meggie, Ronnie and I will. Ronnie can drop her off tomorrow for you. Or you can pick her up."

They talked for a few more minutes and hung up just as Spencer was pulling into his drive way. O'Malley was sitting on her car waiting for him, talking on her phone. She looked better, but he was still mad at his brother.

Spencer had bought the house six months ago. Nicky had told him it was a good deal and helped Spencer with the sale and title transfer. He and Meggie had moved in three weeks ago. He found he was actually excited and nervous for O'Malley to see his home.

When she continued to talk on the phone, he noticed she moved her hands a lot and he noticed that the louder she got, the more the used her finger — the middle one — a great deal. When she flung her phone across the car, he burst out laughing and made her look up at her. In that second, he knew he could love her for the rest of his days.

"That was my CO in Chicago. Commander Hunter said that he has a report telling him I'm not resting, nor am I relaxing. I told him that I had plans to do just that thing very soon. Would you mind helping me with that, Grant?"

She was walking toward him as she spoke. Her body was swaying and moving like liquid sex. He wanted to touch her, to hold her, so bad his body ached.

"I think I can be persuaded to help you with that. You should be naked for this to work, don't you think? I mean, clothes can be so constricting." His voice felt thick, his body heavy with need for her. When she was a foot from him, she stopped.

"Yes, naked is good. So long as you are as well. I was actually thinking we should maybe be that way together. We want to make sure we are both are very relaxed," she purred at him.

"If I touch you right now, we are going to make love right here in the yard. Not that the thought of you beneath me as quickly as possible isn't a wonderful idea, but I have a whole case of condoms and a nice, firm bed in the house just screaming for us to break in."

She looked at him and he felt burnt. Her gaze was sultry and heated. He lifted his hand to touch her face, to bring her closer for a kiss, and she stepped back quickly.

"House, Grant. Now, or the neighbors are going to get the show of a lifetime. I'll pull your cock free and lick you until you come right here."

"Christ," he hissed before turning around and nearly running to the porch. He fumbled with his keys once when she walked up behind him and pressed her body to his back.

"Hurry," she whispered, and he finally got the key in the lock. After two tries, he got the door open, yanked her inside, and slammed the door.

Pressing the lock to secure the door, he pushed her against the wall and lifted her around his hips. His mouth was on hers within seconds after crossing the threshold. Need ripped through him and he wondered how he had made it through the day beside her without wanting her this bad.

He had to have her, be inside of her soon. Without thought of anything other than touching her, he spread his hands along her ribs and then up under her breasts. Her hiss of pain brought him back to his senses.

"Oh baby, I'm so sorry. Christ, I'm such an ass. Let...let's stop and I'll...I can't believe I'm suggesting this, but I'll take you home."

O'Malley stepped away from him and walked to the staircase. As she went, her jacket dropped to the floor. She never turned around, but continued to walk up the stairs. "I'm tender there, but not too bad. You'll just have to be careful when you touch me. I'm not a delicate flower, you know."

Three steps up, her pants slid down her legs and his breath caught in his throat. He watched mesmerized as she leaned against the banister and slipped off her shoes and socks. She put her ankle weapon in her hand.

Taking four more steps, she turned to look at him finally. She stood there in her silk blouse and shoulder holster, a small dark triangle of silk, and nothing more. He swallowed twice before he could get his mouth to work.

"We'll need to find me a place to put these that's close. But if you continue to stand there and drool, I may have to find your bedroom by myself. Are you going to join me, Grant?"

He ripped open his shirt, buttons scattering everywhere, as she stepped up another step. He stripped his belt from his pants and dropped it on the floor next to her jacket. By the time he was one step below her, his shoes were off and his pants were undone.

"The guns, we can slip them under the towels in my bathroom. O'Malley, I'm not going to hurt you, but I'm not sure how long I'm going to last once I have you beneath me. My cock aches to be buried deep inside of you."

"I'm so close to coming, Grant, that I'm not sure you'll get inside of me before I explode. I want you; all this foreplay over the past week has made me too close."

Lifting her up by her ass, she wrapped her legs around him as he gripped her tightly to him. Walking up the stairs with her nipping at his neck was difficult, but well worth it. Taking a left at the top of the stairs, he went to the only door on that end of the house and opened it.

~CHAPTER ELEVEN~

Cait only got a blurred look at the bedroom. It was dark and large was the first impression she got. The second was the bed. It was huge, just like the furniture.

All the furniture was old but well maintained. The bed itself was massive in size both in height and width. It had four posts that looked to have been carved from four-by-fours and cut from solid oak. She knew that the mattress had to have been special made as it looked to be eight-foot-by-eight and as thick as eighteen inches. The soft coverlet beneath her was the softest material she had ever felt.

Cait reached under Spencer's ruined shirt and gripped his shoulders. They were as wide and strong as she had hoped they would be. When her fingers brushed across his nipple, she brought her hand back to rub the light brown circle again and again. Leaning forward, she nipped at the peaked tip and felt his moan move up his chest. Spencer laced his fingers into her hair and dragged her mouth back up to his.

Spencer had the most talented tongue, and it was hot against hers. The way he curved his around hers had her grabbing his shoulders again so that she could ride up and down him using her legs for leverage. She was close to orgasm and they were both still partially dressed.

Cait reached under her arm and with years of practice, undid the closure on her holster and let the entire thing slide off her back. Spencer took it from her and laid it gently on the floor without breaking his mouth from hers. The ankle holster and weapon then lay on top of it.

The shirt she had on was no match for them as Spencer ripped it from neck to hem. It was soon going to be a part of the growing rag pile along with his shirt. Fleetingly, she thought about all the clothes spread out from the front door to this room and started to giggle when he covered her breast with his mouth, nipping at her through her bra. By the time he was crawling to the top of the bed with her wrapped around him, she was clad only in her panties and lacy bra and him in his pants.

He settled between her legs and looked down at her. They were both breathing hard. She knew that he was nervous about her wounds. Frankly, so was she, though not in the same way. She was afraid of what he might think when he saw them. He was probably worried about hurting her.

When he opened the closure in the front of her bra, her right breast was exposed and tight and her left was completely covered in a bandage. She wanted to roll over and hide, but she also wanted to see what he thought. Closing her eyes, she spoke to him. "They told me to take this off...to...to check on it daily and to expose it to the warm air. But I can't...I've not been able...Spencer, tell me what you're thinking."

He didn't say anything. Finally, after several moments, she couldn't take it anymore and turned to look at him. He was looking at her and not the bandage.

"Let me help you, love." Slowly, he began to peel the tape away. It had been working its way loose for a couple of hours now, probably from the heat of her body and sweat. She turned her head away when she felt the last part of the tape leave her skin.

Spencer gently lifted the heavy padding away. The cool air touched her exposed skin and her nipple pebbled. She heard him hiss and his arms tightened around her. She turned to look up at him.

"I didn't realize where they...Damon said that you'd been shot in the chest, but he didn't say...it was close, wasn't it?" His voice was soft, but she could still hear the emotion there.

"Toby Cantel shot me over here first." She indicated her right side. "My lung collapsed and I thought I was dying then. He came at me laughing with the other two cops with him because...I had a reputation for being invincible, which I think he started and I didn't deserve. He thought it was funny that he'd gotten the better of me so quickly. I lifted my gun and when they got close enough, I shot. I shot the first one in the head, killing him instantly. The other cop drew, but I had him down before his gun could clear his holster. Toby thought he had me, you see, and they hadn't expected me to be able to shoot back. Toby had his weapon out and he shot me once more in the chest as I pulled the trigger on my weapon. I missed his head and shot him in the throat instead. As he went down to his knees, he shot again and so did I. His last shot hit me again and mine blew the back of his head off. I didn't...I wasn't sure who I could trust, so I called my uncle and he sent the cavalry."

Spencer didn't say anything and she expected him to...she didn't know what. But what he did next shocked her to her core. He kissed her wounds. Then he said in a voice so heavy with emotion she felt her own tears gather in her eyes and then seep to her cheeks, "You are the most beautiful woman I've ever met. You skin is flawless and so smooth. It's warm and soft. I want to make love to you, Caitlynne."

He laved his tongue over her nipple and then blew his warm breath over it. She felt her entire breast tighten and feel full. When he suckled the hard bud into his mouth, rolling and twisting it with his tongue, she moaned. Cait was nearly ready to throw him to his back and impale herself on him.

"Grant, please. I need you. I want you now. Please?" She had never begged for anything in her life. This was a good time to start.

"I want to taste you, O'Malley. I want to lick your pretty pussy until you fill me with your cream. Then I want to make love to you until you scream with your release."

He moved down her body before she could say anything. Not that she thought she could make a comment. Once he touched her with his mouth, the world around them faded away.

Spencer and his quick tongue whorled in her belly button then took her tiny ring into his mouth and gently tugged. She sat up straight on the bed. Her navel had always been sensitive and since putting the ring there, it was twice as bad. But him using his tongue on her nearly shot her through the roof.

"Spencer, please!" She was begging and sobbing now. Her need for him was making her toss her head back and forth and clutch the sheets to hang on.

Sitting up quickly, Spencer opened his zipper and jerked his pants down. His cock sprang free, a long stream of pre-cum already lubricating the tip of his thick shaft. She leaned forward to lick the bead of cream, but he stopped her before she could.

"You do that and I'm finished. I'm on a hair trigger here, O'Malley, and one swipe of your hot tongue and I'm coming all over you. I want to be inside of you. And putting on the condom is going to be chancy." She giggled slightly and so did he.

It seemed to take the edge off their needs and he reached over her to grab a small foil pack. He got slightly sidetracked when he licked her nipple again and then paused to suckle it.

"Grant, please." She took the condom from him and when he sat up again, she slipped it over the tip and he helped her roll it down over him. Her hands were shaky and she kept fumbling. His cock pulsed in her hand, hot and heavy.

"It's been a while for me, love. A long while, actually. So I'm telling you sorry now if I don't perform up to my usually magnificent self. But I'll make it up to you later."

Laughing, she told him, "Me too. And I don't own any toys to take the edge off. I know that's the new thing, but I don't. But I want you inside of me."

He pushed her back against the pillow and looked at her spread before him. Slowly, he ran his fingers up her thighs and just over her mound. She jerked hard up to his questing finger and whimpered when he made another pass.

Covering her with his body, he pulled hard on her nipple and fisted his cock with a firm grip. Then he lined himself up to the mouth of her heat and nudged her clit with the tip of his cock. She felt her pussy weep heavy for him.

"Please, now. I'm begging you. Fill me, Grant. Now." And he did.

A hard thrust forward and she was stretched taut; her body screamed at the pleasure-pain. Even as he filled her, she marveled at how well he fit, how well they fit. And when he moved inside of her, slowly at first, his face showed the strain he was using not to hurt her. Wrapping her legs around his hips, she shifted and took him deeper.

Digging her heels into his firm ass, she grabbed his biceps and surged up every time he moved downward. His thrusts were firm and hard, getting faster and deeper with every dip into her. She knew that he was getting close when his movements became frantic against her. Suddenly, her climax seized her. It came out of nowhere, tightening her sheath around him. When she screamed out his name, she felt him shift again. He was pounding now, hitting the bundle of nerves inside her with a hard beat that drew her close again. When his fingers reached down between them and he scraped his nail over her clit, she cried out and came again. Suddenly, he froze and even with the latex barrier, Cait felt him come. He shouted out his own release, his voice harsh and long.

Even as her mind and body blurred out, she felt him drop nearly onto her then roll at the last second to the side. He wrapped his arms around her and pulled her over him, his cock still tight inside of her. When he covered them with a blanket, she barely registered it, but snuggled deeper into his warmth.

~~~

Spencer woke with a start to a dark room and nearly rolled out of bed when the woman in his arms stirred slightly. O'Malley. Pulling her tighter to his body, he wrapped one of his legs along her other one and smiled.

Christ almighty, she was wonderful. His cock twitched and jerked when he thought about how she had taken him. Well, he took her, he supposed.

Realizing he still had the condom on, he gently slid out from under her and grinned when she reached for him even in her sleep. With a quick kiss on the mouth, he stood and hurried to the master bath. After disposing of the used condom and washing his hands, he looked in the large mirror over the sink.

He looked like a completely fucked man. He could see the sappy grin and the satisfied look in his eye. Hell, he had seen both looks on his brother's face so much lately that he knew it as well as his own.

He was still standing there grinning like an idiot when Cait's arm slipped around his waist from behind and she squeezed him. He laid his hand over her arm and pulled her closer. "Are you all right? I know for a fact that I've never felt better. You look beautiful, so beautiful," he said when he turned and took her into his arms. She felt right there, like she was made for the sole purpose to fit against him.

"Yes. I feel really good. I'd like a shower before I go, is that all right? I won't be long." She started to pull away, but he tightened his hold.

"Sure. But you're not going anywhere just yet. I still have a full case of protection in there and I've not heard my name but once or twice yet. Stay with me, O'Malley. Meggie is at my brother's and I don't have to get her until late. Please?" He pressed her against the shower stall and began kissing her, not giving her a chance to tell him no. Reaching in behind her, he turned on the taps to the water. When steam started to bellow out, he guided her inside with a press of his body.

Spencer pulled away as the water sluiced over them. He thought she was a little tender knowing he had not really been as gentle as he had wished. He reached over her head for the large sponge and the bottle of his liquid soap, thinking he would have to start buying her things to set next to his. Then smiling, he thought he wouldn't mind her smelling like him. He began filling the sponge with soap as he spoke.

"Tell me something about Caitlynne O'Malley. Anything." He rubbed the sponge down her spine as she bent over and reached for his shampoo.

When she looked back at him over her butt, he wondered how his tongue had gotten so thick and his mouth so dry. It was all he could do not to plunge his now hard cock deep into her opening. Breathing hard, he tried to remember why he couldn't when she started talking to him.

"I had a cat when I was a little girl. His name was Princess Sparky. I'm not sure why right now, other than the fact that I always made him wear this pink tiara all the time. He was a huge cat too. We were inseparable. I have some cousins. Two boys who were all older than me and loved to torment Princess and me. It got so bad one summer day that I walked to the police station to see my dad. I had decided that I was going to file a complaint against my cousins."

"How old where you?" He had moved from scrubbing her back to taking over washing her hair. It felt like spun silk; its heavy mass cascaded down her back in a long, wet coil.

"Five, I think. My dad died when I was six, so it was close to then. He sat me down in one of those chairs across from him and took out a pad of paper and an ink pen. He was getting serious with me, something he knew that I would pay attention to. He started writing things down and asking me questions at the same time. I doubt it was anything more than a duty roster or something, but him putting it on a clip board made it seem so important to me. But it was the way he asked the questions that impressed me. They were standard questions I've asked thousands of times—name of person, Jacob and Timothy Shamus. He asked for their address and I remember looking at him so seriously and telling him he knew where they lived, with Uncle Samuel. Then he asked how I wanted them punished—death by firing squad, poisoned, or hanged. I said that I didn't want them dead, just punished. He told me that when people hurt his little girl, he had no choice but to kill them. That's what daddies did when their little girls filed a complaint. I remember sitting there thinking hard as Princess paced the room. Finally, the big, stupid cat jumped into my lap and looked me right in the eyes. I swear, Grant, I thought he was saying, 'is it really that bad.' 'Maybe,' I said to my daddy, 'you can teach me how to fight back.' The next afternoon he signed me up for self-defense classes. Uncle Paddy made sure I got to every one of them."

He pulled her to him. Even with her back to his front, he knew she was crying. He felt a few tears in his eyes as well.

"I'm sorry, baby. I didn't mean to make you sad. I just wanted to get to know you better."

"I'm not sad. Well, not too sad anyway. I loved my daddy very much. And even though we had very little time together, we lived each day to the fullest."

"I can't believe your dad let you name that poor male cat Princess Sparky. No wonder your cousins made fun of you." She laughed as he hoped she would.

Standing there with the water running over them, she reached behind her and cupped his cock. He moved hard against her hand and need rushed through him again. He was taking his time this round even if it killed him.

Guiding her to the bench in the shower, he gently pushed her forward until her hands rested on the seat. Backing away two steps to look at her, his cock wept a little in anticipation of being inside of her again. But he had other plans.

Dropping to his knees behind her, he ran his hands up her calves to her knees and spread her feet apart. Her pink pussy lips glistened before him. Groaning at her scent, even with the water rushing over them, he leaned in and licked into her heat.

She nearly stood up, but his sharp "no" had her back into place. Moving deeper between her thighs, he pressed his tongue deep into her and lapped at her. Her thighs trembled and while he enjoyed having her open for him, he felt he was not getting as much as he wanted of her. She turned around when he pulled away and he sat her down on the beach, widening her legs as he pushed forward. Cupping her ass and pulling her closer to the edge, he buried his mouth over her.

Spencer had had oral sex before and had enjoyed it. But when O'Malley gripped the back of his head by tangling her fingers in his hair and pulled him hard against her, he nearly came all over the shower floor. Christ, but she was wonderful.

Licking and lapping, he avoided her clit as much as she would let him. He did brush against it with his tongue a couple of times, and she would cry out. The third time he did it; he pulled the tiny bud into his mouth and sucked it hard against the roof of his mouth as he tormented the little slit below it with his tongue. He slid two fingers into her sheath and spread them wide, touching her sweet spot with every pass. She nearly knocked him over with the force of her climax when it hit. Her juices flooded his mouth and he moaned at the taste. He kept fucking her with his fingers and tongue until he brought her to peak twice more in rapid succession.

When she jerked his head away from her, begging him to stop, he stood, turned off the water, and picked her up. Not bothering with towels, he took her to the bed and laid her down. She looked up at him and he pulled out a foil packet and handed it to her.

"Hurry. Please hurry. I need to be inside of you five minutes ago." She had the condom on in record time and lay back, spreading her legs wide to accept him.

His cock jerked hard and he knew he would never last once he was inside of her. Dropping down between her legs, he rocked into her and moaned. Heat, hot as lava and silky smooth, gripped him. Moving out of her to the tip of his engorged cock, he slammed forward and felt her pull him tighter inside of her. Primal need, the need to conquer, to claim, and to mark washed over him and he slammed into her again and again. She surged up with every one of his strokes until he could no longer tell her movements from his.

When he came, he roared out his release. His body spurted and jerked into her, and he knew that he had never felt this powerful of a release before and that he would never again with any other woman. Falling forward, and then rolling to his back, his last thought was that he loved Cait O'Malley.

~CHAPTER TWELVE~

Cait woke to the sound of snoring. It was not a harsh or even a loud snore, but more of an exhausted breathing snore. She smiled as she tumbled out of bed.

It took her several minutes to find her pants and several more before she found her guns. He must have gotten up sometime after they had gone back to bed after their romp in the shower and put them between the towels in his linen closet. She thought about taking a shower, but thought it would wake him and then she would never get out of the house. Moving down the stairs, she picked up their clothing, folded his over the banister, and tugged hers on. She was just walking out the front door when the SUV they had taken from the restaurant pulled up.

"Hi, Cait. I have to get going so can you take Meggie inside? I have a client at the jail waiting for me and I'm running behind," Ronnie Grant said as she unbuckled Meggie from her car seat. Once the little girl hit the ground, she was running toward Cait at full tilt.

"I was just leaving. I have stuff to do today. Can't you take her in? Grant is still sleeping, but he'll get up." She wanted to get going. Cait was afraid to get too much closer to these people, especially the little girl now in her arms.

"I can't. He'll have to take a shower and then get dressed. I really need to get to the courthouse and see my client. Thanks so much, Cait. Tell Spence to call me later."

Ronnie was pulling out into the street when Cait realized that she had said jail the first time and courthouse the second time when talking about her client. She looked at Meggie.

"I think I've just been bamboozled. What do you think?" Shaking her head, Cait walked back into the big house thinking about how best to get back at the lady lawyer without resorting to physical harm. Then she thought about what a perfect pair she and her husband were as lawyers.

Meggie told Cait she was hungry. Cait realized she was as well. She had not eaten much in the way of lunch and she and Grant had not eaten anything once they got back here last night. Cait detoured to the kitchen and hoped that there would be at least a box of cereal in the cabinets.

The kitchen was a chef's dream. That is if the dream consisted of deep walnut cabinets so glossy she could see herself in the shine. The counter tops were a laminate of dark green with specks of deep gold and deeper reds. The refrigerator was a stainless steel doublewide side by side that would have been right at home in most restaurant kitchens. The stove, also stainless steel and as massive as the fridge, had six burners and a grill in the center. The sink was situated in the corner of the room and large picture windows opened the area. The view was spectacular, spilling out into the pool and well maintained back yard. Along the wall sitting on the counter was a toaster, microwave, and something she thought might be a coffee machine, though she was not entirely sure. The island in the middle of the room sported a double sink and a small refrigerator beneath more counter tops, wooden cutting board style this time. Under the island was every small appliance known to mankind and some that were probably not. Hanging over it was a large assortment of pots and pans. There was a large, round crock that held numerous wooden spoons and other kitchen utensils.

Cait was completely and utterly overwhelmed. She just knew that she was not going to find a simple box of corn flakes and that she would certainly make a mess if she tried to cook in here.

"How about if I take you out? I have to tell you, sweetie, I don't do kitchens. I don't even know what half this stuff does, much less how to use it. If you want, I'll get you some waffles or something." Meggie was already shaking her head. Cait was so screwed.

The first thing Meggie did was pull out a small step ladder and open a cabinet that slide out and revealed a large assortment of cook books. She pointed to them as if to say, "You can read, can't you? Then you can cook." Getting the not so subtle hint, Cait pulled the first one off the shelf only to have Meggie put it back and hand her another one.

This one had pictures of kids cooking with an adult on it and Cait thought the child leaning on the counter looking at her was too smart for her own good.

She opened the book and started reading. Okay, maybe she could do this. How hard can it be if they let you make...crepes with kids? Getting out the ingredients, they began their adventure.

~~~

Spencer could smell it when he woke up. He was not sure what it was, but thought it had to be from outside. He was disappointed that Cait had gone, but knew that she would not get too far. Smiling, he stepped into the shower and then dressed quickly.

The closer he got to the kitchen, the more worried he became about what he thought was coming from outside. The smell...burning eggs, he thought, and it was coming from his own house. He stopped when he heard Cait talking.

"I don't think this is right either. And stop laughing at me. This was your flipping idea. I wanted to go out, but no, you had to hand me a cookbook instead. I bet the next time your aunt suggests you stay with me, you'll say no."

Spencer realized that Meggie was in there as well. He leaned against the door jamb and listened more. He was not worried about his kitchen; anything she might have done he was sure he could clean up. And if he couldn't, then he would simply buy a replacement. He nearly laughed out loud when Cait started again.

"See what that picture looks like? Does this even resemble...stop laughing at me, young lady. Your dad is going to kill us both. Oh yeah, both of us. You too! I'm going to tell him this was your...it was too. Shit! I mean shoot. It'll take days for this to come off this pan.

And there aren't any more eggs either, thank goodness. Now can we go out to eat? I'm starved."

Spencer opened the door and stopped dead in his tracks. Okay, maybe it would be easier to move. The kitchen was a mess. No, beyond mess; it was a disaster. It looked as if every pan, every bowl and every utensil had been used at some point and tossed toward the sink. The dishwasher was open and it looked like it had been filled by tossing things at it from across the room, and no food had been scraped off. Every burner on the stove was on and the oven light was bright as well. The island, his pride and joy, was covered in egg shells and empty cartons. There was a stack of cold toast that looked like it had been an entire loaf of bread with the butter now congealed on the slices. Glasses were everywhere and there was a mild spill on the floor near where Meggie sat perched on her ladder still in her jammies. Cait was dressed in one of his dress shirts that hung to her mid-thigh and her dress pants.

"I'm guessing we should have gone out to eat, Meggie. Your dad looks like we just took his favorite toy from him and broke it. I can explain, Grant." She looked ready to cry, something that shocked him more than the mess in the kitchen.

"I hope so, though I don't really care. What is it you were trying to make anyway? A bomb? It looks like it was successful if it was supposed to blow up in the kitchen and resemble a food fight."

"Ha Ha, very funny. Your sister-in-law dropped off Meggie just as I was leaving. She said she had to go see a client, but I think she was trying to be sneaky for some reason. Anyway, Meggie hands me a cookbook and we set off. I'm afraid I have no talent for the kitchen."

"No kidding. What were you trying to make anyway?" He looked down at the Cooking with Children cookbook and nearly laughed out loud again. "Easy Crepes" was the title on the page. He wondered what she would do to him if he told her Meggie could make these without any problems, had in fact made them for him on occasion. He winked at his daughter.

"I should go. I've really...I'm sorry about this, Grant. I wanted to cook her something, and it seemed easy enough, but it isn't." Cait started backing toward the door and he stopped her by pulling her into his arms for a kiss.

He wasn't sure how much longer or how much further they would have gone if Meggie had not clapped her hands. Grinning at Meggie, he kissed Cait again.

"You are not leaving me with this mess. Both of you are going to clean this up, starting with the dishes. Meggie, you load the dishwasher and show O'Malley how to do it. I'll start on the counter tops. Then when I find them, I can cook us something...well, anything else. All right?" When they nodded, so did he. "Good."

Spencer watched the two of them together. Every time Cait put a dish in wrong, Meggie would take it out and hand it to her again. It wasn't long before Cait got the hang of it and Meggie was patting her on the back. Once the dishwasher was loaded, Cait filled the sink with soapy water and pulled a chair over for Meggie to stand on so she could dry. The counters may have gotten finished faster if he didn't keep catching himself just watching them, but it was just too beautiful of a sight to see Meggie laughing again.

Meggie hadn't been born deaf. Meggie's mother, Shannon, had let an ear infection go too long before seeking medical treatment for her. By the time Meggie saw a doctor; she was in severe pain and had to be hospitalized for the infection. But that was not the whole of it. Shannon had had a live-in boyfriend who hated children and when Meggie's cries had kept him awake one too many nights; he had slapped Meggie repeatedly on her tiny ears and shattered her ear drums when she was only three months old. Then last year, Shannon had decided that she didn't want to be a mother anymore and had "sold" Meggie to him.

When he found enough counter space to cut things up, he pulled down his favorite skillet and put it on the burner. With a few pats of butter sizzling, he started cutting up carrots, onions and garlic. It was nearly lunch time anyway and he decided to make a quick stir fry with the left over rice and a few fresh vegetables. The aroma soon took over the smell of burnt egg and filled the house with a much better scent. Finding some chicken left over from yesterday's lunch, he cut it into long strips and then tossed it in with the veggies and garlic. By the time he put the rice in the skillet, the girls were finished with the dishes and were setting the table.

"Five minutes, ladies. Let's see if we can get the coffeemaker going too." He noticed that Cait had never drunk coffee before, and was not surprised when she declined to join him for a cup.

No one said anything as they started eating. Spencer felt bad when he realized that Cait hadn't eaten since yesterday and had been watching Meggie for three hours before he had finally come downstairs. But other than the kitchen, neither of them seemed to have minded the time alone.

"What are your plans for today, O'Malley? Want to hang out with Meggie and me? We're going to the mall to shop for a Memorial Day outfit for me. I think I'll wear a pink tutu and a short skirt."

"I have to go soon. I'm headed back to Chicago tomorrow and I still have to pack. But I would like to see you in the tutu. Can you send me a picture?" She was smiling, but it never reached her eyes.

Before he could ask her to stay, his phone rang. He reached out and took her hand when she started to get up. It was several seconds before he realized he missed something in the phone conversation.

"I'm sorry, what did you say? I've got company here and I was distracted."

His office was being moved; could he come to the university and talk to the dean? He understood that the building where his office was stationed was being renovated, but why was the dean involved? Spencer had been a tenured professor at the university for nearly sixteen years teaching History. He was also on vacation, his first since he had gotten out of college and started teaching.

"Dean Williams would like for you to meet in his office as soon as you can, this morning if possible. He said he has some things he'd like to discuss with you before term starts next fall," the woman's voice told him again.

"I have my little girl right now and I can't leave her. My sitter is on vacation as well. I'll have to call you right back, all right? I need to call one of my family members to take her."

"What's going on, everything all right?"

He looked at Cait and found he wanted to cry. He couldn't very well talk her into staying when he had to go to his office. "I have to go to the dean's office and see what he wants. I have to call my mother and see if she can watch...crap! The caterers will be in today. Maybe Morgan. I wonder if she can take…"

"I'll keep her. That is if I don't have to cook. She and I can go over to my uncle's house and hang out. She likes him okay." Meggie loved Paddy O'Malley, actually, and they both knew it.

"No, I don't want to impose. Besides, there's the shopping thing. I promised her a trip to the mall. And it's not just for an outfit; she doesn't have any summer stuff."

"I know how to go to the mall, Grant. And I can promise you she'll be safe with me. I won't cook anything for her at all even if we are both ready to eat the other's legs."

Spencer looked over at Meggie. She was nodding her head so hard that he was sure she would get a stiff neck if she kept it up. It was then that he realized that both he and Cait had been speaking to each other and to Meggie with sign as well.

"Okay. But I pay for the trip. Here, let me write down her sizes for you. I don't know what's in the mall for a little girls' stuff, but I'm sure she does. Morgan took her there for her birthday last year and spent a fortune on her. Are you sure about this?"

"Yes. We'll be fine. I need to replace my aunt's blouse anyway. It seems to have gotten torn somehow."

After he programmed his cell phone number into her phone and gave her the sizes and his credit card, Spencer called the secretary back and told her he would be in soon. Cait and Meggie loaded up in his new car and headed to her uncle's house so Cait could change. Spencer drove to the university and thought his face was going to hurt tomorrow from all the smiling he was doing today.

~~~

Cait left Meggie in the kitchen with her uncle and aunt and went up to take a much needed shower. She thought she had flour in her bra and she felt a little sore from last night. Standing under the hot spray, she realized what she had done.

She had spent the night with a man and now she was watching his little girl for the day. And not only that, but she was taking her clothing shopping. Cait had to lean against the wall while she took several deep breaths. What the hell was she thinking? She knew it had to do with his sex appeal, at least sleeping with him part, but the kid? Muttering under her breath about needing her head examined, she got out of the shower and started to get dressed.

She didn't have a lot of clothes with her, a few pairs of jeans and a couple of pretty tops. She hadn't planned to stay long when she'd come here, just get well enough to be able to protect herself then move back to her tiny apartment. Pulling out a pair of fresh pants, she was putting them on when she thought about her apartment.

Cait had moved in just out of college. It was a nice enough place if one overlooked the fact that she lived within spitting distance from the elevated trains. The noise was so much a part of her that she had had a hard time getting any sleep when she had first moved here. There was a single living/dining/kitchen room that was open and airy. Her furniture was nice, though she rarely sat on it. The kitchen table had one chair, which was good as she only had one plate, two forks, a spoon and a knife. She did have a great many paper plates and plastic ware to round off if she needed more. She drank neither hot tea nor coffee so she didn't have a mug. The coffee pot had been a gift and she had never even plugged it in. The refrigerator had a drawer where she threw all the packets of whatever sauces came with her take out — mostly soy and hot mustard and nothing much else. It was thankfully empty when she had gotten hurt or she would have a hell of a nasty mess when she got back. The couch had been a hand-me-down from her uncle's house and the only time it was used was when she forgot to put sheets on the bed or fell on the couch when she was too tired to go to bed. Her bed was a single and the sheets were as old and worn as the rags her aunt Dee used at home. But it was hers.

She found Meggie in the kitchen telling her aunt the story about the cooking disaster from this morning.

~CHAPTER THIRTEEN~

"How much do you know about shopping? Because I have to tell you, kid, I know next to nothing. I know how to buy my underwear and stuff, but I know diddly about buying for a little girl," Cait told the little beauty in the back seat.

The mall here in Columbus was huge and according to the map in the front entrance, was well equipped for just the kind of shopping they were there to do. Problem was, neither Cait nor Meggie knew that much about fashion.

"Okay. Here's the plan. We'll sit in the food court and make notes on what you like and don't like. We'll be on a kind of stake-out. You see something you like; we'll note it—colors too. I don't know about you, but I've heard that some people can't wear certain colors. And, of course, we will snack like crazy."

The two of them sat at a large four top table, ate their way through every restaurant, and wrote down all the things Meggie liked. Cait even saw a few things for herself. Two hours later, equipped with full bellies, notes on clothes, and names from shopping bags, they hit their first shop.

"I don't know about this one, Meggie. It looks a little odd, don't you think? I mean, is it supposed to hang like that?"

Meggie had picked out a bright green shirt thingy. It had a tie-dyed t-shirt under this vest/sweater thing that twisted into a knot in the front. It looked neat on the mannequin, but neither of them could figure out how to put it on a real person.

"I think it's broke. And how the he...heck is a person supposed to get into it if you wanted to dress yourself? Maybe we should skip it and try something else. If we can't figure it out here, your dad is never going to get it."

"Want some help? Come here, sweetie, let me show you both." Morgan stood behind Cait and had nearly startled her into pulling her gun. She turned slightly and looked up at her from her position on the floor.

In two moves and a simple twist, Morgan not only had the thing looking like it should, but also better than it looked on the doll. Cait was still on her knees in front of Meggie and as soon as Morgan was finished, Meggie stepped closer to Cait and put her arms around her neck. Cait held her to her. She never thought of herself as a hugger, but Meggie could certainly make it worthwhile.

"Did Grant send you here to check up on us, Mrs. Grant? I told him that I'd watch over her. He didn't need to make you come out." Cait could hear the hurt in her voice and felt herself blush with it.

"He didn't. I had no idea you two were going to be here today. The boys need some summer shorts and shirts and while they're at preschool, I thought I'd get it done. If Spencer had a problem with you watching Meggie, you wouldn't be here with her. And my name is Morgan."

"I'm sorry. I'm not...I'm not very good with this stuff. I don't know anything about kids and less about...thanks for your help. We were just finishing here and moving on to the store at the other end of the mall. Then we were going to get some more lunch. Would you like to meet us there? I mean, if you don't have..."

"I'd love to. Margaret is supposed to meet me here at three. Would it be all right if she joins us? She has some things to pick up and we meet for lunch whenever we can."

Cait turned to Meggie to see what she wanted to do. Both women had signed when they spoke. Cait did it out of habit and she was glad that Morgan seemed to have no problem with it either.

"Okay. Meggie and I will meet you at the restaurant at three o'clock." Then Meggie and she went up to the counter to pay.

They would not take Spencer's credit card, stating without him there and the amount she was spending, it was against company policy. So Cait paid for the shopping spree. Smiling as she put her credit card away, she was thinking about ways to make him pay her back—all three hundred and fifty dollars of it.

The next store had more frilly things than either female was comfortable with. The entire store looked like a vat of pink paint had been spewed on the walls and clothes and even the carpet. Meggie made the comment that they would need to wear sunglasses if they ever came in again and Cait agreed.

Meggie was looking at a pink wind breaker when she suddenly stiffened and whimpered. Cait immediately gathered her into her arms and stood. A beautiful woman stood just behind them and when Cait took a step back from her nearness, she took one forward.

"What the fuck are you doing with my daughter? I want you to give her to me right now or I'm calling security. Meggie, come with me right now." This must be the infamous Shannon Grant.

Meggie gripped Cait's neck tighter and cinched her legs around Cait's chest wound. She would worry about what she had done to the area later. She was more concerned about the fear Meggie had for this woman.

"Meggie is with me. And she's not going anywhere with you without Grant's permission. Who are you anyway?" Cait knew, but figured she would keep that to herself; Meggie looked a great deal like the woman.

"Shannon Grant. Spencer is my husband and he told me to pick her up today here. How else would I know you were going to be here if he hadn't told me?" She started to reach for Meggie again and Cait twisted around so that she could not touch her.

"You reach for her again and I will have you arrested. I'll call Grant and ask him. Now, you'll back the fuck up or I'll back you up."

Cait pulled out her cell and looked for the number Spencer had put in her phone. She knew immediately which one was his; he had called himself Granite Hard Lover. She pressed send and waited. Frowning when she was told the number was incorrect, she tried again. Same. Damn it.

"He didn't give you his number? Oh that's perfect. Well, since you can neither deny nor verify my claim on my own child, then I'll just take her."

Cait didn't know what do to. Meggie obviously didn't want to go with her mother. Cait had no doubt that she was who she claimed, but that could be for any number of reasons. But Cait knew in her gut that Meggie was not supposed to be with Shannon. Thinking about the consequences, she took a chance on erring on the side of caution and pulled her weapon out while she pulled Meggie behind her. And waited.

She didn't have long. Shannon started screaming at the top of her lungs the moment she saw the gun. Screaming that Cait had kidnapped her daughter, and that Cait had tried to rob her, anything to get attention on them — and attention was just what they got and what Cait needed.

When the mall security showed up, Cait dropped to her knees and presented her weapon to them. She held it with her thumb in the trigger guard and it hung loosely down. Neither man would approach her. Which was fine by her. It was according to standard procedure as she was armed and they were not. Meggie was also still hanging on to the back of her shirt and looked as if she was not going to let go anytime soon. The police arrived five minutes later. They had no problem approaching and taking her weapon.

"I'm a Chicago Homicide Detective here on medical leave. My badge is under my shirt and I have another weapon on my left ankle. This woman is claiming to be this little girl's mother and is trying to take her from me."

"You couldn't work it out any other way than to draw your weapon, Detective? You know, talk it over like friends? Anything else? You know I have to take you in and verify this..."

Shannon started yelling about stupid cops and ignorant lawyers, how just anybody could carry a gun and that she was going to sue everyone standing there. The officer turned back to Cait with a wink.

"Ah, I see now. You thought your way might be safer. Probably right. Okay, gents, load 'em up. We're all going downtown."

Cait smiled when she heard Shannon cursing the officer who was trying to lead her to the car. Cait had pulled her weapon so she was handcuffed, but so long as Meggie was close, she really didn't care. When they put her in the back seat, Cait watched the younger officer try to reason with Meggie.

"She's deaf. If you lean down where she can see your mouth, she'll understand you. Ask her mother to translate for you if that doesn't work," Cait said, trying to be helpful. Meggie was sobbing and trying to get to her.

"I have no idea what she's saying. I never learned that crap. If she wants to talk to me then she'll learn how to talk like a real person. With all of Spencer's money, he should have had her fixed by now."

The officer holding on to Meggie's hand looked at Cait. It wasn't hard to read the expression on his face. He was appalled by Shannon. Without saying a word, he opened the back door to his cruiser again and helped Meggie in with Cait.

~~~

Spencer's head was reeling. He had just been made head of the History department. Not only did it come with a much bigger office, but he now had a secretary and a small budget for staff. He was sitting in his new office when his phone went off.

"Doctor Grant?"

"Yes. This is Spencer Grant. What can I do for you?"

"My name is Tyler Cort and I'm with the Columbus Police Department. Do you have a daughter? And can you tell me the last time you saw her?"

Spencer's heart skipped several beats and he had to clear his throat several times before he trusted himself to speak. The things roaring through his head were dark, bloody and scary. Meggie, his little girl, was hurt.

"This morning at around eleven. Is she all right? Please tell me. I'm leaving right now; just...please tell me that she's fine." Spencer was leaving his office and out the door before he realized that something had to have happened to Cait or she would have called him. "The woman, Caitlynne O'Malley, is she hurt too."

"Everyone is fine, sir. There was an...an altercation at the mall and Detective O'Malley was brought in for questioning. Your daughter is here with us, but we don't have permission to let her go with anyone else. Your mother is having a hard time adjusting to that, by the way, and the rest of your family is...I don't suppose you could come down here and rescue us, could you?"

Spencer leaned against his car. An altercation at the mall was not even close to what had been running around inside of his head. He grinned when he thought about his family ganging up on the department, especially his mother.

"Yes, I'm leaving right now. Can you tell me what the altercation was about, Officer? I may want to leave them all there for the night."

"Seems your wife and your girlfriend had a fight over the little girl."

~CHAPTER FOURTEEN~

Cait lay on the bunk in her little cell and thought about what was going on. Not just with today, but the whole visit. She'd only come here to rest and now she was in a jail cell because her lover's—no, her married lover's wife had demanded her child back. In the two weeks since she had been in Ohio again, she had nearly gotten herself killed in a car crash saving Meggie, been operated on, spent three days in the hospital, had sex, gone to the mall, been arrested again. And now here she was trying to figure out if said married lover needed to be shot, castrated, or allowed to explain. Right now, she was leaning heavily toward the first two.

"Detective? Your bail has been paid. You can go now." Officer Cort had been the arresting officer and also the one who had put Meggie in the car with her. He had grumbled all the way to the station about unfit mothers and their stupidity until he realized that Meggie could see his face. He flushed.

"Thanks. Do you know who paid it? I have to make sure they get paid back, you understand," she told him when she stood. Cait had been fighting dizziness since she had left the mall. The police had already checked her wounds, at least the one on her ribs, but she knew that the other one, the higher one, had been hurt too. But there was no way she was baring her breast for a bunch of cops she did not know.

"Yeah, Doctor Grant. He's waiting for you upstairs. That other one, the ex-wife? If she ain't a piece of work, I don't know what is. Them Grants, they can stick together like nobody's business, can't they? When that older lady showed up, I thought the captain was gonna let you go just to get rid of her. What a fubar."

Cait agreed, Fucked Up Beyond All Recognition. She turned and looked at the young officer. She didn't know whether to laugh or hit him. They were in the squad room now and there were several civilians around who could hear every word he said. He either didn't care, or was trying to make her laugh. Either of which was inappropriate. Before she could comment, a small bundle of little girl hit her in the legs.

Dropping to her knees, she hugged Meggie. She was so glad she was all right that she felt tears prickle at her lids. Cait looked up when a shadow moved over her.

"I'm thinking the mall isn't safe for you either. Or would that be you aren't safe for it? Are you okay, O'Malley? You look a little pale," Spencer asked her.

"I hurt, but I'll be okay. Do you think you could drop me off at my uncle's? I'm whipped and I want to take another shower. Oh, and your car was dropped off at your house earlier. My Uncle Paddy took it—"

His mouth covered hers in a quick but powerful kiss. She didn't know what to say and thought before she said something really stupid like "please do that again, only longer this time," she kept her mouth shut. But she never stopped clutching his shirt.

"You are going to my house. I'll drop you off to get some clothes, but after that, you and I are going to talk. The first thing is why didn't you call me when Shannon approached you? I could have verified that she doesn't have Meggie and—"

"Now you just hold on one second, buck-o. I tried calling you. You did something wrong and it said the number was not assigned to anyone. And how the heck was I supposed to know you were married? You didn't mention that part when you had your dick inside of me. I will not be treated like a bimbo, buddy. And I will not be ordered around by the likes of you." She gave him a hard shove and walked away.

She gathered up her things from the duty officer and stormed out of the station. She was so mad that it took her a few seconds to realize that she had no way home. Grumbling and bemoaning her lot in life, she took off walking. She was perhaps six blocks away when a car pulled up beside her. If it had have been Grant, she would have ripped him to shreds. But it wasn't; it was Damon who rolled down his window to talk, but did not get out of his car. He was a smart man.

"I'd like to examine your wounds if you don't mind. I know you hurt; I could see it in your eyes when you tore out of the police station. I'll take you wherever you want to go after that." She glared at him.

Cait didn't know if he was trying to hide his laughter or what, but he was doing a piss poor job of it if he was.

"Did he send you? If he did, then you can go on back to him. I'm a big girl, Doctor Grant, and I don't need nor do I want someone breathing down my neck."

"It's Damon. No, he didn't send me. I, too, make my own choices. Now get in and I'll even examine you at your uncle's house if it makes you more comfortable."

She did. It was either that or fall on her face. Exhaustion was beating at her and the more she tried to fight, the harder it got to be to do so. By the time they were pulling onto her uncle's street, she felt better. A couple of times, she heard his cell phone go off and after looking at the screen again, Damon turned off the thing and put it back in his pocket.

"He's not going to be happy about you not answering him. In the short time I've known him, I've noticed that he is a tad controlling. What's he going to say when you tell him you're with me?"

"Plenty, I'm sure. But he'll get over it. My mother is going to call you later. She is very mad at Spencer herself and wants to apologize to you. She told me to tell you that she raised us better than to act like Spencer did toward you tonight."

"Tell Mrs. Parker not to worry about it. I'm sure he'll forget me soon enough, but she has no reason to be upset with him. We just had sex, nothing more."

"Yeah, we all got that part. You should know that Shannon and Spencer aren't married and haven't been since Meggie was an infant. She was never any good before they married and she didn't improve with time either." Damon snorted and continued, "I tell you when you get your temper up, you sure are a sight to behold, aren't you?"

She flushed when she remembered what she said to him about his dick and the fact that they had had sex. Cait was not sure about what sort of sight she had made, but she was aware of the fact that she had embarrassed herself and probably a good many other people as well.

"Shit! Your mother was there when I...damn, damn, damn! I swear that my temper never gets the better of me. It's just that...that he...fuck!"

They went into the house and while Damon talked to Paddy, she went to her room to change. She wanted to shower and scrub the jail smell off her, but wanted to get the exam over with and get Damon out of the house. She had had enough of the Grants and was not particularly happy with one of them right now. When she went into the living room again, she nearly turned around and went back to her room.

~~~

Spencer stood up when she walked in. Christ, she was good and mad. And beautiful. It didn't take a lot to see that she was barely holding on to not shooting him right now. He swallowed twice before he trusted his voice.

"I wanted to say I'm sorry. I screwed up. I—"

"No. What you did was fuck up—royally. Now get out. I've had about all I can take of you tonight and I hurt. So unless you have no desire to ever have another child, I suggest you leave."

"Meggie isn't mine. I knew that from the beginning, but I didn't say anything. Not to anyone. When Shannon said she was pregnant, I knew she didn't love me, but I thought we could make it work. I was getting to the point where I felt it was time for me to get married so I stupidly went into it with the thought of changing her. The only thing I managed to do was make us both miserable. Then when Meggie got hurt, I knew it was over. Shannon's boyfriend—she had several of them by then—he hurt Meggie because she wouldn't stop crying. Then six months ago, Shannon sold Meggie to me. Shannon gave up everything for money and she was never to contact nor have anything to do with her again. I'm sorry I didn't tell you about her. I had no idea...that's not true. I hoped she would just walk away and leave us in peace. I'm sorry, Caitlynne. Please forgive me."

Spencer watched as Paddy and Damon walked out of the room. He had never told Damon what he knew. A few months after Meggie was born, he'd taken her to another doctor to make sure. He had hoped that...not that it mattered then or now. Meggie was his no matter what the DNA test said.

"You embarrassed me. In front of you mom, you embarrassed me. I tried to call you...that stupid name...she tried to take Meggie from me and she was so terrified. I didn't know what else to do. I wasn't sure if she was...she told me she was your wife and that you sent her to me."

He started toward her slowly. He wanted her to take her into his arms, to hold her and to comfort her. Spencer knew that he had screwed up, royally, as she had said, but he wanted to make it right, to get her back.

"I'm sorry. Come home with me, please? Let me make it up to you. I'll make you breakfast in bed. Meggie and I will pamper you all day tomorrow at the picnic. We'll celebrate. I got a promotion today. I want you to celebrate with us."

He was close enough to touch her now. Slowly, he lowered his head to hers. Her breath felt warm moving across his lips. And when she licked her lips, he didn't even try to hold back his groan.

"What about tonight? Who will pamper me tonight, Grant? I've had a very rough day. And you owe me. I had to spend my hard earned money because your credit card wouldn't work. Are you going to try and figure out a way to pay me back?"

He spread his hands over her ribs and gently pulled her closer. Brushing his thumb under the curve of her breast, he felt it swell and tighten. Moving his hand down her hip, pulling her closer still, he bent at the knees, cupped her ass, and lifted her against his erection. Her back arched and she pressed her soft folds into his shaft. Christ, this woman could make him needy faster than anything he had ever known.

"Come home with me. I want to make love to you all night. I want to taste every inch of your delectable skin then I want to start over and taste you again. Please, baby. Come home with me right now."

Not waiting for an answer, he took her to the door. He started kissing her as he pressed her against it while he fumbled with the door knob. Her mouth was hot and open under his; their tongues mated and tangled together until he wasn't sure who was seducing who.

"We have to slow down. At least until I get you to my house. Shit! Meggie is at the house with Morgan. She was going to get her ready for bed and then wait for me. I'll call Damon when I get there; it'll keep me from throwing you to the floor and taking you before I can get rid of Morgan. If there's anything else that requires a great deal of thought, I don't think I'm capable of answering right now. There isn't a drop of blood anywhere but in my groin — which, might I add, is a constant state of erection when I'm around you."

She giggled. Caitlynne O'Malley, Homicide Detective, just giggled. He wasn't sure, but he thought that was by far the sexiest thing he had ever heard.

~Chapter Fifteen~

Spencer looked over at the woman on the couch with him. Cait had pulled Meggie into her arms the minute she had walked in. Not even when her favorite aunt left would Meggie leave Cait's arms. Now they were all together on the couch, watching television.

Morgan had not stayed long when they finally got here tonight. She offered to take Meggie home with her, but Meggie would not go. For as much as he wanted Cait, having his daughter close was suddenly important to Spencer. He didn't want to think about what would have happened if Shannon had succeeded in taking her today.

"This is not really how I planned to have you tonight. A six-year-old can really cramp one's love life." But he found he really didn't mind. Cait was here and they were together.

"She's asleep, poor baby. It's hard shopping for summer clothes and almost being kidnapped. And you — you look very tired too, you know. Maybe when you take her up, I'll go home. You need to get your rest—"

Cupping the back of her head, Spencer pulled Cait to him and kissed her. Her mouth was delicious and he wasn't sure he could get enough of her. But one thing was for sure, she was not going home tonight.

Breaking off the kiss, he stood up. Looking down at Cait, he noticed her nipples were hard and that she was breathing hard. Moving toward the front door, he began locking up the house.

"I'm going to see to the house then I'm going to take Meggie to her room. She'll sleep all night, but you are not. In fact, you'll be lucky if you get any sleep at all. I'm going to ravage you. Then when I'm...where are you going? You shouldn't be lifting her." He moved toward her and stopped when she raised her hand.

"If I take her to bed, you can finish up down here. Then you can take me to bed sooner. I'm quite capable of lifting a small girl. The thing you should be worried about is if a man your age can keep up with me at my full strength." He watched as she turned and walked toward the steps. Cait was completely out of sight before he got his mind moving again. Good Christ, she was going to kill him. Smiling, he finished locking up the house and setting the alarm.

The light to his room was on when he got to the top of the stairs. He looked down the hall and saw that Meggie's door was ajar and there was a little light spilling out into the hallway. Cait must have turned on the night light for her. He went into his room and noticed the bathroom was being used and that his bed had been turned down.

Spencer realized he was nervous. This was not like before when they were nearly tearing their clothes off each other to have sex. This was...this was making love. He was going to make love with Cait. He started to sit on his bed, but then thought that seemed too desperate. He was walking around the room and straightening his things when he heard the door open behind him. When he turned to look at her, he knew that this was beyond making love; this was being in love. He loved O'Malley.

"I don't have a lot of clothes here. And the last time, well, the last time we were kind of rough on them. I hope you don't mind. I was going to just wear a t-shirt, but you don't seem to have any of them."

She was in one of his white dress shirts. The sleeves were rolled up to her forearms and the hem hung just to her mid-thigh. With the light of the bathroom behind her, he could see that she was braless under it and decided that he would never wash that shirt again.

"No. I don't mind. I'll replace your aunt's shirt. You look very good in mine. Though I'd like it better if it were on the floor next to the one I have on."

The light went off and he realized she had lit the couple of candles he had. They had been in Meggie's room; he remembered seeing them when he was looking for her sweater yesterday. The glow looked romantic.

"I've never...this is different than before. With you, I mean. I know that I...I want you, but not like I did before. Am I making sense?"

"Yes. I was thinking the same thing. Come here. I want to undress you." She started toward him, but was shaking her head.

"Not this time, Grant. This time, I want to undress you. And I want to taste you. I want to make you so hot for me that you beg me to let you fuck me. Then I might relent. But tonight, this night, you're mine." She stood in front of him.

He couldn't breathe. He was sure he was, because he was not passing out, but he was dizzy. Reaching up, she pulled the clip from her hair and it fell to a heavy tumble of curls to her waist. Her breasts strained against the buttons when she lifted her arms in much the way his cock did against his zipper.

"Don't touch me unless I say you can. I want to be able to touch you without you taking over, understand? I want to taste and bite you wherever I want without you trying to stop me."

"Yes," was about all he could manage as she unbuttoned the top button of his shirt. He had long since taken off the tie, but he was still buttoned to the top. When her lips touched his collarbone, he moaned and moved his head back for her. When his hands touched her hips, she pulled back and he dropped them again. He was not going to make it and she had only kissed him once.

"Your skin tastes like warm sunshine," she said as the second button came open. "And you smell like sex to me. I never thought of sex having a smell, but you have it." The third and fourth button opened and she widened his shirt enough to lick a path to his nipple. Her bite was almost painful, but erotic too.

"Are your nipples sensitive, Grant? I can't wait to nibble on your cock. I won't hurt you; I'm not into pain, but I would like to nibble a little." The buttons were all undone, but she didn't move to remove his shirt from him. When she walked behind him, running her fingers along his shoulders, he whimpered.

"O'Malley, you're killing me. I want to touch you. I want to taste you too. Please?" Her long fingers ran up his neck from his shoulder to his hair line then up over his skull. Tingles of need raced along his blood stream and he thought he could come from just her touch.

"Not yet. I want to play. When I first saw you in the hospital, I remember wondering how broad your shoulders were and if I could hang onto them when you fucked me. I was actually shocked by that thought. And now look, I not only know they're strong, but that I need to hold them when you're pounding into me." His shirt slid off his shoulder and down his arms, the cuffs trapping his hands. Cait didn't unbutton them to free him, rather tightened them together in a cuff that held him in place.

"O'Malley, you know that I'm going to make you pay for this, don't you? That for every minute you make me suffer, I'm going to double it for you."

"I hope so, Grant. That is, providing that I don't kill you first." She was in front of him again and this time, she pressed her hand against his erection, cupping him tightly in her fist. "I want to suck you. I want you to come down my throat like you did before."

His cock was throbbing now and he could feel the liquid staining his pants. When she unbuckled his belt, he had to take deep breaths to regain control of himself. She must have sensed how close he was because she paused with him. When he nodded to her, she continued.

The belt came off quickly; she must have known that much more and he was going to spill his seed without her. He watched as she dropped to her knees in front of him and unbuttoned his pants and then lowered the zipper slowly. When she was halfway down, she stopped to kiss the exposed skin.

"O'Malley!" He was not beneath begging at this point. He was not going to last more than ten seconds once her hot mouth covered him. Spencer felt his knees wobble and tremble. His cock sprang free and he moaned. He looked down at his cock and watched as a thick stream of cum leaked from the tip. He wanted her to lick it off, but knew if she did, he would come; that was how close he was to his limit.

His pants were down around his ankles when she stood up. He thought she was going to leave him standing there, but she started to unbutton her shirt quickly. When the shirt joined his on the floor, he growled. She was naked.

"Let me go. Please, O'Malley, let me go so I can fuck you. I want to come in that hot pussy of yours."

Instead of answering, she dropped to the floor again and pulled him into her mouth. His body surged into the wet heat. While her one hand pumped him, her mouth sucked hard at his bulbous head. When her free hand slid up his thigh, he knew that he was going to come soon, and as soon as she cupped his balls, he did.

With his hands tied behind him, all he could do was pump hard into her. Her head moving up and down his shaft and her moans urged him on until he emptied himself into her. When she let go of his cock, she leaned back and he could see her glistening pussy open wide. His cock twitched at the sight and he knew that he had to have her.

"Let me go. Now, O'Malley. Untie me." She looked at him, dazed, and as her fingers trailed along her thigh to her pussy, he almost let her go so that he could watch her. "No! Don't touch yourself. Let me go. Right now, let me go."

She looked at him and he turned around. As soon as the shirt slipped free of his wrist, he turned around and scooped her up by lifting her under the arms. As soon as her body touched his, his cock jerked to attention and she wrapped her legs around his waist. When she began sliding up and down him, he stopped moving toward the bed and savored the feel of her bare heat on him.

Pulling her away, she whimpered when he pushed her back on the bed, and she started to reach for him again. Backing away from her touch, he grabbed a condom, tore the foil package open with shaky hands, and rolled it over his swollen cock.

"Lie back and spread your legs for me. I want to watch you play with your pussy while I recover. But don't come, not yet. I just want you to play."

"I'm close, Grant. I need to come, I'm so close." Her fingers opened her folds and her clit looked swollen and hard. He wanted to take it into his mouth and suckle it, but he knew for as good as it would feel to have her come in his mouth, his cock needed to be inside her.

"No, I'm going to fuck you hard. And when you come, you are going to scream my name for me. Scream it until you're hoarse, understand me?"

"Hurry," she said, and opened her legs further and planted her feet on the bed. Every swipe of her fingers over her pussy, she would surge up a few inches off the bed. Finally, when she touched her clit, she moaned deep. He watched as her juices seeped from her as she thrust two of her fingers from her free hand into her pussy, fucking herself.

Kneeling on the bed between her legs, she looked up at him as she continued to play. Her breasts were heaving and flushed with need. He fisted his rock hard cock and moved it along her fingers. She ran her wet fingers along his tip and pulled him to her opening. Dropping over her, he slammed into her as hard as he could, filling her and stretching her.

Grabbing his shoulders, she clawed down his back and screamed as she surged up with her release. His body rocked again and again, each time she tightened around him, milking him and pulling him deeper. Her second climax had her digging her heels into his thighs as she tried to hang on. When his own release hit him, he pumped into her, short, hard jabs until his emptied himself again.

He dropped onto her when he finished and buried his face into her neck. He promised himself he would move as soon as he caught his breath. He knew he was heavy and probably crushing her. He didn't remember falling asleep.

~~~

Cait woke to a phone ringing close to her head. The tone was familiar, but her fuzzy mind could not place it. She tried to reach for it, but the heavy body lying across her was not helping. Lifting Spencer's arm, she slid out of the bed and onto the floor. The room was chilly on her bare body, but she grabbed up his shirt and tugged it over her head as she went to find her pants. She was too late to catch the caller, but needed to go to the bathroom first. She left the bedroom and stepped into the hall when her phone rang again.

"O'Malley. And this had better be good to call me at four-thirty in the fucking morning, you asshole. I'm on leave, remember?" She heard her captain, James Britain, grunt, his version of saying he was sorry, and smiled. She like the old curmudgeon and actually missed him. Too bad her CO was not like this man.

"Martinez is getting out on bail. His bail will be set at ten million, but we both know that don't mean squat to him. Judge called me this morning and let me know. I tried calling your house and your uncle said you were getting your whistle wet. What the hell does that mean? You finally getting laid, O'Malley?"

"Fuck you. How long do I have? 'Cause I'm sure you didn't call me to tell me it's happening today, did you?" She looked down the hall and saw Meggie coming out of her room.

"On the fourth. You come back here and you might as well sign your own death certificate. Stay there and maybe that uncle of yours can help. I got no one here I trust yet. What is it you wanna do?"

Four days was not a lot of time. Four days for her and untold time for Martinez because she had no doubt he had been working hard at getting her dead.

Anthony Martinez had been arrested right after she had been shot. What they had on him was slim at best and she was surprised that he had been held this long. The gun that Toby had used on her was registered to Martinez, but there were no prints to tie the gun to him other than that. He claimed that the gun had been stolen and he had not reported it because he didn't know until the police had shown up at his door.

"The trial wasn't set yet when I talked to you last. Anything on that yet? And do we have anything else to go on?"

"Trial has been set for June tenth. His passport has been taken and his plane grounded. As far as other evidence, yeah. I was able to track down the warehouse, but as you can probably guess, it wasn't being used when we went in. It was funny how it was clean as a nunnery and all but blessed when ATF came in. We do have the records, the ones that you found and the ones we got from Cantel's house. The three witnesses we have, one is you, and the other two are dead. I don't suppose you know any more."

"No, not yet. I need a throwaway and a connection. I can take care of the rest. Uncle Paddy doesn't want me to leave and the captain here is all right. Give him a call for me and set me up. Don't talk to anyone but him though. I've not had any contact and don't want to start something here my ass can't pay for."

"O'Malley, watch your back. You're a good cop, better detective, but a pain in my ass that I've grown to like."

"Yeah, back at you, shit face. I'll talk to you in a couple of days." Cait was sitting on the top step when Meggie sat down next to her and laid her head in Cait's lap.

"Oh, Meggie. I'm in big trouble here. I've fallen in love with your daddy and I'm going to get myself killed. What's a girl to do?" Cait knew that Meggie could not hear her and that was the point. But she did need to get her to bed. Picking her up as gently as she could, Cait carried the little girl to her room.

~CHAPTER SIXTEEN~

Spencer woke up and reached for Cait. Sitting up when he felt nothing but cold sheets, he looked around the room and noticed that all her things were gone. Checking his watch, he realized it was much later than he had planned to wake. Rolling out of bed, he went to check on Meggie.

Her room was empty. Well, that wasn't quite true; there was no one in there. But he could see that someone had been a little busy though.

Three of the big boxes were now stacked against the wall near the door, empty. There were still five or six left yet to unpack; he was still happy. Walking further into the room, he looked at one of the big bookshelves and saw that many of Meggie's books were now stacked on the shelves and a lot of her breakable toys now graced the middle shelves. Another bookshelf had dollies and stuffed animals on it. He smiled when he noticed that they were stacked by color, animal and size. He knew who had started on this shelf. O'Malley was organized and maybe a little OCD.

Meggie's bed was made in the way of a child, covers tossed in the general direction of the bed and pillows half on and half off. Spencer noticed the trash can had hangers sticking out and walked over to see what else might have been tossed when he saw store tags. Shopping. Cait and Meggie had been shopping for summer clothes. Deciding everything was all right, he went back to his room and showered and dressed. He smiled all the way down the big staircase and into the kitchen.

"Good morning, ladies." They were both sitting at the kitchen table with the TV on but muted with closed captions. Meggie was eating some of the most colorful cereal he had ever seen and Cait was having a glass of water. He kissed Meggie on the head and drew Cait up out of the chair to kiss her too.

"Good morning. I was hoping to wake up before Meggie and make love to you again. What time did she get you up?"

"I got up around four-thirty; she got up around then. We had a nice nap after we worked on the boxes in her room. That was okay, wasn't it — to put her stuff away? She told me that the decorator was in but left without finishing her bedroom. Meggie said she was tired of tripping over them."

Spencer looked at Meggie, who was completely entranced in the show she was watching. He pulled Cait closer and kissed her full on the mouth. She tasted minty and fresh. Her tongue was warm and he wanted to have more of her. When she moaned deeply, he realized how much he could come to enjoy having this daily.

"I have to talk to you. My captain called this morning—no, my CO. He's the reason I woke up. Martinez will be getting out on bail in a few days, on the fourth. His court date is next Thursday and I need to be there. It would be safer for all of you if I…"

He didn't want to hear this and decided to kiss her instead of listening. He knew that eventually it would no longer work to keep her distracted, but he enjoyed trying. She pushed away from him and frowned up at him.

"Listen, this is serious. Martinez is dangerous and we need to keep diligent. Captain Britain said that I need to get with the captain here and make sure that everyone is ready. Martinez is a very dangerous man and he wants me dead in the worst way. I have to be gone before he gets here and uses any of you against me."

Spencer didn't want her to leave. He was afraid if she did, she wouldn't return. But he also knew that she was in danger and with her, them. Frowning, he looked at her.

"What do we need to do? I can learn to shoot, and I know that most of my brothers can already. I think it's a good idea about your uncle and the police force. The more we have working...why are you shaking your head no? You can't think I'm going to allow you to go...O'Malley, don't get your panties in a twist. I didn't mean that the way it sounded."

He knew better than to try and order her around, but he wanted to protect her. He also knew that in a pinch, she would be the one to do the protecting no matter how much he wanted to think otherwise.

"I do not get my panties in a twist, Grant. And you would do well to remember that in the future. I'm trying to tell you that I can protect myself, but I can't protect everyone."

His house phone ringing startled them both and he went to answer it. He knew she was not finished with him and by the look in her eye; it wasn't going to be pretty. He smiled when his mother was on the other end.

"You know I said to be here at ten. It is now noon. Was there a breakdown in communication somewhere, or am I just getting senile in my dotage?"

"No, ma'am. I'm sorry, I overslept. The good news is Meggie and O'Malley are already dressed and I just need to grab some shorts. We'll be there in twenty minutes. Can I bring anything?"

"I don't know what you just agreed for me to go to, but the answer is no," Cait whispered angrily at him. He grinned and nodded. She glared. It was never going to be a dull moment with her, he thought.

"No, just get your butts over here. And tell Caitlynne O'Malley that I heard her and that if she does not show up with you then I will send her uncle after her. He showed up on time. And her lovely aunt Dee has been very helpful."

"Hum, Mom, maybe you should tell her. She is none too happy with me right now. Here." Spencer shoved the phone at Cait and walked away.

Cruel? Of course. But he was only protecting himself from both women. When she got off the phone, O'Malley wouldn't even look at him. Gathering up Meggie, she went to the car and got them both in.

Spencer counted himself a lucky man; he was out of harm's way and his mother was happy.

His family had a Memorial Day picnic every year since he had been a little boy. The guest list got longer and the guests more prominent with each passing year. It was mostly because of his brothers and their pursuits.

His brother, Devin, was thinking about running for District Court Judge next term. And Ronnie's parents, Austin Pride and Ben Kendal, were already considered the richest men in the United States by most financial magazines. Nicky was also looking into politics. Byron had become more famous over the past few years, and his guests alone had a sheik and two lords.

As soon as they pulled into the yard, they could smell the food. Roasting hog had been going since very early this morning. Large tubs of ice were loaded down with soft drinks and bottled water. There were several open bars set up with a bartender at every one. Food was also in abundance, though most of the dinner items — corn on the cob, potato salad, cole slaw, and different breads would not be out until it got closer to dinner time.

Spencer came around to the passenger side of the car and grabbed Cait from behind. She had been unbuckling Meggie and he pulled her against him for a quick kiss and to press her tight against him.

"Don't be mad at me all day, please? I'm sorry about this morning. I never meant to make you mad. I worry about you and want to be the he-man and protect you. I know that you will probably be the one that will have to save the day, but it doesn't make me want to save you any less."

"I'm not a girly girl, Grant. I'm a grown woman who can and has been taking care of myself for a long time. Please take this seriously. I don't want anyone to get hurt," she told him as she leaned back against him.

"I know, and I will. The mayor and the chief of police are here today, as are most of the other officers. Maybe you could talk to them now."

She said she would and turned to finish getting Meggie out of the car. That was when he noticed how she was dressed. Both of them.

Meggie had on a bright green pair of shorts and a bright pink top that had swirls of the same green as the shorts splattered all over it. Her hair was pulled up into braids that had the pink and green ties at the ends and ribbons at the top. Her sandals were pink with green flowers on them. She looked so adorable that he wanted to pick her up and nibble on her. Her cheeks were red from her excitement and she was smiling hugely at him.

O'Malley had on a dark green sleeveless knit shirt and a darker green short sleeve sweater over it. He could see her shoulder holster when she moved, but the cut of the sweater kept the gun from being too obvious. A wide belt wrapped around her waist. He was sure if he looked, he would see her extra clips and a few other things attached to the back of the belt somehow. Her Capris were a dark denim and fit her body like a glove molding over her curves and making his mouth water. She had on a pair of white tennis shoes and no socks. Her hair, normally pulled back in a tight bun, was in a very loose braid that hung down her back and was tied at the end with a pink ribbon. Meggie had put that there, he was sure.

"Meggie, you look beautiful. Did O'Ma...Cait help you pick these out?" When she shook her head at him, he looked at O'Malley. "I don't remember seeing these in her things from her mother."

"She picked them out. Not me. Well, except for the shoes. The lady at the store said they would go with a lot of her outfits and Meggie let her talk her into them. I don't care for them myself, but then I don't have to wear them. And just so you know, she calls me O'Malley too."

Meggie asked to go show her grandma her new clothes and she was off. A year ago, Meggie would not have left his side for anything. Then Morgan had come into their lives and she and Meggie had become friends.

"I don't think I thanked you properly for taking her shopping for me. I think I probably still owe you some of the money you spent on her too. Want to come back to my house after this and let me make another payment to you? I think I could make a big dent in what I still owe you."

She shuddered when he ran his tongue along her jaw and down her neck to just behind her ear. He loved touching her and could not seem to get enough of it. When he pressed his mouth over hers, she opened under his and sighed into him. Pulling her closer, he felt her second gun at the middle of her back and a pair of magazines right where he thought they would be — right along the belt.

"You two might want to pace yourselves. You have your whole lives ahead of you. Mom wants to borrow Cait for a little while and I need to talk to you." Jamie had turned his back on them when he spoke.

"Can't you just tell her you couldn't find us? You could tell her that we dropped off Meggie then drove off like a bat out of hell. Grant and I will corroborate your story."

Spencer thought it was a great idea himself. Right now, he was trying to figure out a way to get O'Malley up the stairs and into his old room without anyone noticing them. But Jamie was not going to help.

"Okay, first, I don't lie to my mom. Even though I know I'm a grown man, she still scares me. Secondly, I don't cuss at her either. She'll rip my hide off me in two seconds flat. One look from her and I'm a puddle. Go to her, Cait, before she comes looking for me to see why I haven't told you she wants you."

With a "scardey cat" from Cait, Spencer kissed her, and off she went to the kitchen. He caught himself watching her walk away and then saw that Jamie was doing the same.

"Hey! Eyes off, she's mine. What does Mom want with her anyway? Oh God! She doesn't want her to cook something, does she? O'Malley is, by far, the most competent woman I know, but I swear, Jamie, she is a kitchen moron."

"Nah, I think she just wants her to help put food out or something. I actually think it's a ploy to get to know her better, but I could be wrong. I just heard about your promotion, congratulations."

"Shit, I completely forgot about it. You haven't told Mom yet, have you? If she finds out before I tell her, I'm dead."

Spencer was afraid of his mother too. Not that she would hurt any of them, or even anyone for that matter. But she would be hurt and that would be much more painful than her physically hurting them.

"No, but I did want to talk to you about your old job. I want it—and your office. I've been at the university for seven years now and I'm about due for the tenureship."

Spencer and Jamie each taught at OSU. Spencer had been there nearly twice as long, but Jamie was quickly making a name for himself as a fair professor and a great teacher. Spencer knew that if anyone could do a good job as head of the department, it would be him. The two men talked about the pros and cons of working with each other the rest of the evening whenever they were together.

~~~

Cait walked into the kitchen and started to turn and leave when Margaret yelled at her to come back. Damn it, she was going to have to shoot somebody today; she just knew it.

"You are going to come in here with us and keep us company. Now, sit there and I'll give you some vegetables to put onto this platter. I've already heard about your lack of cooking skills so we won't give you anything that you can hurt someone with," Margaret told her as she placed a huge platter in front of her.

"Very funny. And I don't know how to cook because I choose not to, not because I'm lacking the ability to learn. I'd like to see any of you shoot a target from fifty feet and hit it dead center mass every time." She was being bitchy, but Margaret had started it.

"Well of course we can't. Why would we? Now, tell us about meeting the whore from hell the other day. I have to tell you, I wish I had have been there when you pulled that gun on her. She has always been a bitch and probably always will be. So tell us."

So, Cait told them how Shannon Grant had tried to take Meggie away from her and what had happened afterwards. But the end of the day, Cait was glad she had come along, but she had no intentions of telling Grant that.

~CHAPTER SEVENTEEN~

The ride back to Grant's was quiet. Meggie had fallen asleep well before the fireworks and had slept right through them. After they were over, Margaret had given them several plastic containers of leftovers to take back with them. Spencer seemed fine with it; Cait didn't care. She was almost as tired as Meggie at that point.

After putting her to bed, Cait went back downstairs to the kitchen to put things away when she found Spencer had already finished up. She wasn't sure what to do. She didn't want to just go up to his bed and she wasn't sure she should go looking for him. So she sat down at the table and straightened up the papers lying there. She was so tired that she laid her head down and before she knew it, she was asleep.

When she woke up, she was in Grant's bed. He was lying next to her, well actually, he was lying on her, but she found she didn't mind. His body was big, but since she was not a tiny person either, they fit well.

She thought about what was going to happen over the next couple of weeks and knew that she needed to get away before someone got hurt. She didn't know what she would do if they got hurt because of her. Looking over at Spencer's face, she realized that she was in love with him. She was still staring at him when he opened his eyes.

"Why do you look so sad, baby? Come here and let me hold you." He stroked her back and held her. She felt the tears stinging her eyes and was afraid they would fall on his chest and he would be upset with her. When he ran his finger along the necklace at her throat, he pulled the little ring out and looked at it.

"My father gave it to me. See, it's a cuff key. It was his and for my fifth birthday, he had it made into a ring for me. He told me that all cops had one, a hidden key on them to open cuffs if they were ever trapped by them. He told me that it would be very embarrassing to be found locked in your own cuffs." She showed him how the little flower moved back and the key exposed itself. She looked up at him when she felt him staring at her.

"I have to go to the university today and finalize my paperwork. I don't want to, but I have to turn it in by Monday morning if I'm going to be able to take over the position by fall quarter. Would you like to come with me? I hate to say it, but it will be boring as hell and Meggie might get antsy. But I'd love for you to come if you want to."

Yes, she did want to spend the day with him, but not in public. She understood about wanting to get the paperwork finished. She had heard the pride in his voice when he had told his family about his promotion at the picnic and didn't want to stand in the way of him doing what he wanted.

"No, Meggie can stay with me. I have some errands to run yet. And some things I have to do at my uncle's house. I also have to meet with Captain Tucker. He has some equipment for me from Chicago. We'll probably spend the day at the house. Why don't you come over there when you're finished and have dinner with us? Aunt Dee loves to cook and she's quite good at it."

"All right. Sounds great. But right now I want to make love to you. Somebody fell asleep last night and I didn't get to make a payment. Why didn't you just come up to bed anyway?"

Instead of answering him, she kissed him as she moved him to his back. She didn't want to tell him she wasn't sure what she was supposed to do, nor did she want to assume she had any rights in his house or his bed. He seemed to like her there, but she still didn't want to overstep her bounds.

"I want to ride you, Grant. I want to feel your cock deep inside of me while I move over you. Please?" Cait spread her legs over his waist and leaned down to nip at his nipples. She knew that he liked her biting him and enjoyed listening to him moan when she did it.

He put his hands on her thighs and spread her wider. Her panties and a t-shirt was all she had on and she wondered if he had been hard when he had undressed her. Reaching down to the bottom of the shirt, she pulled it up and over her head and tossed it to the floor.

When his cock was between her legs and her pussy over it, she leaned forward and rode him. He surged up and his cock pressed hard against her clit and she moaned. The panties had ties on the sides that kept them in place and when she felt his hands gather in the material, she stopped him with her hands.

"Don't. They untie. I'm running out of under clothes since I met you. And if you keep this up, I'll have to go commando until I get back home." He tore them from her with a growl and she felt her pussy gush over him.

Looking down at his cock, it glistened with her juices. All she could think about was watching him come this way. She wanted to see his cock jerking as he came. When he shifted under her, she stilled him with her knees. But he was stronger and he flipped her to her back.

"O'Malley, I need you. I want to fuck you from behind in the worst way. Roll over and stand up."

Her body shivered at his command and her pussy wept more. She could feel her juices gather on the tops of her thighs. She stood near the large post at the end of the bed and watched as he opened a packet and rolled it over his length.

"Lean over and hold onto the post. That's it; now spread your feet wide. Oh, baby, I can see you, all of you." His finger was suddenly inside of her, deep and hard. She nearly moved away from him and would have if he hadn't put a hand on her back to stop her. "Don't move. I want to touch you. Have you ever had anyone in your ass?"

"No. Never. I don't...I don't think I'd like it. You're too big, Grant. Don't."   His hand coming down hard on her ass startled her and she started to turn and hit him back when he slapped her ass again. It felt...good. Painful, but very good.

"Don't ever tell me no, O'Malley. Not in here. You can be the big bad cop on the outside, but not in here. Understand?" She didn't know if she liked him telling her no either, but when his hand came down twice, three times more, she knew that she would do anything he wanted.

"Please."

"You going to let me fuck you in your beautiful ass? I won't hurt you, but I want to try." He fucked her pussy more with his fingers, now there were two. Her body creamed him and she felt him move his finger up her crack to her tiny hole. She tensed when he ran a finger over the area.

"No, don't tense. Let me love you this way. I'll move easy. That's it, baby, relax."

At first, he just pressed hard against her opening, using her own juices as a lubricant. When he moved his finger in past the tight muscles, she heard him moan deep in his chest. It burned slightly, but soon that gave way to incredible pleasure and he had only just begun. Soon, she was pressing back against his hand and when he brushed his cock against her pussy, she opened her legs wider.

"I'm going to fuck you like this because my cock is about to explode. But I'm not going to stop working you open for me." His cock slammed into her pussy at the same time he pressed a second finger into her. Her climax ripped through her.

Never had anything ever felt so good. He pulled his cock out to the tip and slammed again, ramming his fingers deep into her hole again. She let go of the post and put her head on the mattress; she couldn't hold on any longer.

Grunting his approval, he slammed again and his fingers dug again. Suddenly, he hit a spot inside of her and she went off again, screaming out her release. Cait knew that she had taken him with her; his body was slamming hard into her and he was yelling out her name as he spilled his seed. When he finally fell against her bent body, he took them both to the bed and rolled them to his back. His cock was still deep inside of her as she lay over him.

Breathing hard, he moved her to her side and spooned in behind her. She didn't care if they ever moved again. Sated and relaxed like she had never been, she fell asleep again. She barely remembered him getting up once, then moving her to the center of the bed, but as soon as he snuggled up behind her again, she went back to sleep.

The next time she opened her eyes, Meggie was in the bed with her watching TV. The sound was off so it hadn't bothered her. When Meggie noticed that Cait was awake, she reached over to the side table and handed Cait a note.

"Meggie woke when I left so I told her to stay with you. I should be finished up around six and I'll meet you at your aunt's. I think I left my cell at my mom's; I'll call yours with my office number as soon as I figure it out.

S"

After letting Meggie know she was going to take a shower, she got up and found her clothes again. He had put another of his shirts on her. She didn't have any panties, of course, but after taking another of Spencer's shirts, she went to the bathroom.

She was a little sore, she noticed, when she bent to pick up her clothes. In the past week, she and Spencer had had sex more than she had had in four years, maybe longer. But it was worth it.

After getting Meggie dressed and making the beds, she gathered up her things and drove to her uncle's. It was nearly nine-thirty and her aunt and uncle were just finishing breakfast, but Aunt Dee made them something to hold them until lunch. Cait was surprised to see that the equipment from her boss in Chicago had arrived at the house and she got busy setting it up. By lunch, she had what she needed.

"Uncle Paddy, Martinez has been busy. This has gone beyond what we found at Toby's house. He is into child pornography, it seems, as well as drugs and prostitution. I wonder just how far reaching this really is. What I found today was simple to locate."

"Do you think he is getting sloppy? Or has he just gotten to the point where he thinks he's untouchable? You said yourself that he has most of the cops in his pockets. Toby couldn't have been the only one on the force that worked for him." Cait had already thought of that and so had Tucker. The problem was, who?

"He goes up for his bond hearing in a few days. I'm not sure what will happen, but I have a pretty good idea. Britain wants me to stay here — the jury is still out on Hunter. I've already contacted Captain Tucker and he is offering me his complete support. He also suggested that I be careful with his cops too. He said as far reaching as Martinez is; there is no reason to think that he hasn't contacted some of his men too."

"You know I got your back. I think you should stay here at night—just until this is over. During the day all of us are a tad more...focused. At night, well, things could be a little distracting."

Cait flushed. She knew she was an adult and her uncle had always been very up front with her, but talking about her sex life with him was just a little too much. But she did agree. Before she could say anything, the house phone rang.

"It's Tucker. Sounds kinda pissed off. Said he's been trying to reach you all day. Your phone on, Caddy-did?"

Before answering, she pulled her cell out and realized that it had been turned off. She wondered about that, wondered if Spencer had shut it off so she could sleep. But it mattered little right now. When it booted up, she had several texts and voicemail.

"He's out! Christ, woman, I've been trying to tell you all day. I've been to that Grant's house, his office at the university, and there is no one there. I finally had to go to the archives and get your uncle's address and number to call you here."

"Who's out? Martinez? You said it would be days yet. Damn it, when?"

"I didn't find out until nine this morning. I don't know what happened, not all of it right now anyway. He was being transferred to the county seat in Chicago when there was an accident just after five this morning. Two of the men in the transport were killed and three others injured. It took them two hours to figure out he wasn't in the van."

She looked at the clock. It was just after eleven. It took at least seven hours to drive here from there, which meant she had less than two hours to get ready. She had no doubt that he was coming for her.

"I'm coming in. I don't want...Tucker? Are you there? Shit! Uncle Paddy, we have to move, now!"

She pulled out her weapons and checked the magazines. She opened the bottom cabinet, moved the hidden wall, and pulled out three vests. She tossed one to her aunt and tugged one over her head as she ran. Running into the living room, she scooped Meggie up into her arms. The vest was too big for her, but Cait had not ever expected anyone as small as Meggie to ever be in the house when something went down. She rushed to the garage behind her uncle and aunt.

When Cait had been a teenager, her uncle had made them practice evacuating the house every week. He was a homicide detective and knew that sometimes — most of the time — people were not happy when you put some of their crew behind bars. The garage was an arsenal and had a great escape vehicle.

The car was an old police car that she and her uncle had modified just after they bought it. The engine had been rebuilt and revved up and the doors and floor boards had been reinforced with two inches of steel. It was bad on gas, but it was as safe as they could make it. They were headed that way now.

The first shot came from the left and Cait fired that way, hitting the first man in the head. He went down quickly. Paddy was just behind her car, firing at someone to the right, and her aunt was firing with him. Tucking Meggie behind her and having the little girl wrap herself around her body, Cait stood and fired twice more at the man across the street. They were not going to make it to the garage.

~Chapter Eighteen~

Cait was trapped behind the door to the garage when she heard her uncle cry out. She couldn't move to go to him; Meggie was clinging to her leg and there was a person firing at them from just beyond the house. She knew she had to stay focused, but her heart ached with the knowledge that she had brought this here.

The man firing at her finally popped his head up and she fired and got him in the head. When she was sure that she could move, she pushed open the door and slipped her and Meggie inside. Moving to the wall and pressing the code, she opened the safe, took out all the clips, and put them into every pocket and crevice she could find. Pulling another automatic out, she put it in her pants. Moving to the car, she opened the door and put Meggie in the slot in the back seat.

"I'm so sorry, baby. But you need to stay in here until someone takes you out. I'll get you to your daddy, I promise. I love you, Meggie. And I'm so sorry." A hard hug and kiss later, and Meggie was as safe as Cait could make her.

She went back out into yard and was hit. Her arm exploded in pain, but she didn't stop—she couldn't. Lifting her other arm, she fired three times into the wood at the corner of the house and a body dropped. Making her way to the car where her aunt and uncle were took eight minutes.

The second man came around the house near the deck and opened fire on her; she was hit once more in the chest, but the vest stopped the bullet from entering her body. She managed to wound him, but he moved out of her vision before she could finish him. Moving faster now that Meggie was safe, Cait ran to the front of the car and dropped next to her uncle.

"Glad you could join us, Caddy-did. Meggie safe?" She handed him four of the clips she had gotten and two to her aunt. A man moved into her sight just before she could answer, and she killed him.

"Yes, in the car. Aunt Dee, can you get to the car? Don't open the garage door, but drive out through it. Go to the station. I'm hoping Tucker is sending in some back-up, but I'm not sure who we'll get. Go only to Tucker, understand? Uncle Paddy, are you all right?"

"I'll cover you both. You go with them. I've got enough ammo now that I can hold them off if they try to follow. Go."

Cait looked down and saw that he had been hit in the belly. He had been trying to hide it from Aunt Dee, she realized. She was no more leaving him than he would have her and they both knew it.

"I'll stay. I'm sorry, Uncle Paddy. I never thought..."

"You stop that right now! You are my niece and I can't think of anywhere I'd rather you be than right here with me. You dinna do nothing but the job you'd been hired to do. Your daddy would be proud of you, standing up for what's right. Hell, he's probably crowing to anyone around looking down on us. You keep focused and we'll get out of this."

When her aunt was ready to move, Cait stood and drew fire on herself while Dee ran to the garage. Cait managed to kill one other person and that's when she heard the sirens. When the car started in the garage behind her, Cait felt a little lighter.

The men trying to kill them doubled their efforts and opened fire on the little car she and her uncle were hiding behind. Two men rushed them and she was able to stop one, but not the other, and he was about to fire on her when her uncle moved in front of the bullet.

She felt the impact into her own vest as it went through him. He lifted his weapon and fired twice more and killed the man who had gotten within four feet of them. Paddy moved off her, crawled to the left, and fired once more before Cait could move again.

The bullet had hit her in the chest, this time in the wound from earlier. The pain was crushing and it stole her breath away. She lifted her arm only to have it fall again. She felt paralyzed. Cait looked at the garage door and wondered when her aunt was going to come out when another man moved toward the door. Moving in a sluggish manner, she fired twice and then had to reload. He went down, but again, it was not a killing blow.

Turning toward her uncle, she could see a trail of blood where he had moved away from her. She started forward when Martinez stepped out of the garage door. His arm was bleeding. Just as she raised her weapon again, she noticed that Meggie was standing in front of him and he had a gun to her head.

"You fire, she's dead. I'm going to walk away from here, but first, I'm going to kill you. You have been a pain in my ass for too long." He raised his weapon.

"Police! Halt!" The cavalry had arrived, but too late. His gun went off and everything went black.

~~~

Spencer pulled up as far as he could and leapt out of his car. He was running to the roped off area at full speed when a cop stopped him by grabbing him around the waist, taking him down.

"My daughter, please, my daughter is there at the O'Malley house. Is that where this is? Please, you have to tell me."

"Doctor Grant? My name is Captain Tucker with the Columbus Police Department. Can you come with me?" Tucker lifted the yellow tape up and Spencer froze. If this man knew his name then it had to be at the O'Malley house.

"Is Meggie all right? And the O'Malleys, are they...Christ!" Spencer stopped and looked at the carnage.

There were seven white sheets lying around the street where he and the captain were walking toward an ambulance. There was blood staining each one. He didn't look too closely, but he thought that they were all head wounds. The closer he got to the squad; he saw two more near a car.

"Detective O'Malley has been shot, and we are getting her ready to transport. She has been... Spencer didn't hear anything else as he rushed to the back of the ambulance.

Cait was sitting on the bed and there was blood all over her. She was crying, but seemed to be all right. As soon as she saw him, she moved out and into his arms. He could feel her crying and kissed her head.

"Where's Meggie, baby? They haven't told me anything, but I don't see her." He let her go when she pulled back.

"He took her; Martinez took her. I'm not sure —"

"What do you mean he took her? You were supposed to keep her safe. You told me...no, you promised me you'd watch over her. How the hell did he get her?"

"Doctor Grant, they had —"

"They? You mean you and your uncle couldn't keep one little girl safe? Christ, and to think that I trusted you." He grabbed her shoulders and shook her. "If so much as one hair on her head is harmed, I will take everything you have away from you. Do you understand me? Everything. You and your family. You'll get her back for me and you'll do it right now." He pushed her away from him and she staggered. Had not the captain been there, she would have fallen.

"All right, Gr...Doctor Grant, I'll get her." Cait turned, handed the padding she had in her hand to the man in the ambulance, and moved away.

Spencer watched her walk away and sat down on the step into the ambulance. His head was spinning and he was sick to his stomach. Meggie was kidnapped and not by her mother, but a murderer.

"What the fuck have you just done? Do you have...come with me." Captain Tucker grabbed Spencer by the arm and pulled him across the street to the car where two sheets were laid out over bodies. He tried to pull away, but he was no match for the very pissed off man.

"Look at him. Look at the man lying here dead." When Spencer didn't move, Tucker reached down and tore the sheet off the body. "He took nine bullets. Nine, you fucking bastard. Paddy O'Malley was a good man and didn't deserve this."

Tucker threw the sheet back down and pulled Spencer along toward the garage. He was sure he didn't want to go any further, but he was too numb to fight now. Tucker didn't even ask this time, but pulled the sheet back on the other body, this one in the garage near a car.

"This woman couldn't even hear her assailant. She took three bullets and from what we can tell, she probably hit the man who shot her. Cait told us that they had Meggie in the car and Dee was going to make a run for it. You said you were going to take everything Cait had, including her family. Well, I got news for you, you fucking ass wipe, her family gave everything they had, including their lives, to protect your daughter and you just sent Cait to her grave." Without another word, Tucker walked away.

Spencer dropped to the floor and stared at Dee. She had two bloody stains on her chest and he could see the bullet hole in her head. He was still sitting there when a uniformed officer came up and asked him his name.

"Yes, I'm Spencer Grant. Is there any news...have you heard from Detective O'Malley yet?"

"Yes, sir. She called the captain and told him she knew where Martinez was and that she would contact him when she was sure he was there. Captain Tucker said I should take you home; there wasn't anything you could do here."

Spencer couldn't go home. He had to be there when Cait got Meggie for him. He knew that she would too. She would do whatever it took to get her back. But at what cost to herself, he wasn't sure. He nodded to the officer and stood. He pulled out his cell and called his mother.

"Mom, Meggie's been...Cait, she's hurt, and I...Paddy is dead and so is Dee. I hurt her, Mom. I sent her to her death. And now Meggie has been taken and I told Cait she had to...Christ, Mom, I need you." He was sobbing now and had to lean against the wall for support.

"We'll be right there. We just heard on the news about the shootout. They're saying that twelve are dead and three are injured. Everyone is here and I'm rounding them up right now. Spencer, she'll get Meggie back for you. I don't know all that's going on, but I'm sure that Cait will make her safe."

Spencer was sure she would too. And with getting his daughter back, he would lose Cait too—one way or another.

~CHAPTER NINETEEN~

Cait walked as far as she could then finally had to sit down on the sidewalk. Her head felt as if a jackhammer was pounding inside and her chest hurt to breathe. The wound in her leg had been wrapped by the ambulance attendant, but she had had to remove it when it soaked through. Her dark jeans did a better job of hiding the blood than the padding did stopping the bleeding. She looked toward where she had come from and noticed the trail of blood. Shit, that can't be good, she thought with a giggle.

She needed to get to the bus station downtown and then to the drop car she had placed when she had been able to move once she got to Ohio. But the way she was losing blood and as dizzy as she was, she would never make it to either place if she tried walking. Pulling out her cell phone, she dialed the taxi service.

They told her it would be ten minutes and she spent that time reading the text messages that had piled up and then the voice messages. There were four messages from Spencer that she saved and two from Captain Tucker. He had left her his phone numbers, including his home and cell, and she thought she might need them later. The rest she deleted. The texts were mostly from Tucker. Though he had basically left the same information on voice mail, she still kept them. By the time she had finished, the cab pulled up.

The ride to the bus station was not long, but it was enough time that Cait could rest. She took inventory of her weapons and ammo and then of herself.

She had three full clips left and both her weapons and one that belonged to her uncle. She wiped furiously at the tears that fell when she thought about his and Aunt Dee's death, but knew that she had one more thing to finish before she could mourn them. Meggie would be home for supper or Cait would die trying, and there was a good likelihood that she would.

She had a bullet wound in her leg that she had gotten when one of the wounded had fired at her when Cait had tried to move closer to the garage. The bullet had gone through, which was good, but it had been in the large muscle in her thigh and hurt like hell. The wound in her arm was not so bad, just a graze about three inches long. It probably needed to be stitched close, but she wasn't worried about it right now. She was afraid to look at her chest, especially after she saw the face of the ambulance attendant when he had removed her vest. He had told her that she was going to need surgery again, and that he was surprised and impressed that she could move at all. So was she, actually. The bullet wound in her head hurt the most. Martinez had fired at her from such a short distance; she knew he could not miss. But Meggie had jerked him, Cait had seen, and thrown his arm off. The police pulling up was probably all that prevented him from firing again at her.

The wound was just at the right temple and had laid open her head from there to the back of her skull. She knew from past experience that head wounds bled a lot, but this was more than that. Cait was seeing blurry and she was constantly fighting dizziness. Being sick to her stomach and heaving whenever she stopped to rest didn't help either. By the time the cab pulled up in front of the bus station, she had rested enough that she was able to walk in without anyone noticing her.

When she had first gotten around to coming here, it was the middle of the night and it had been busy. Now it was the day after a major holiday and it was fairly quiet. She moved to the lockers as she pulled out her key. Locker twenty-four was still closed and her things, thankfully, were still inside.

Pulling out the heavy duffle, she took it to the bathroom and went into one of the larger stalls. She hated to use the handicapped one, but she had to change her clothes and fix her leg and needed privacy and room to do so. Besides, she thought, she could not get much more handicapped than she currently was. She nearly giggled again, but stopped it before it could pass her lips.

The first thing she pulled out was the first-aid kit. It was one of the larger ones and she knew that she could repair most of the damage that she could see with it. Opening it up, she pulled out the scissors and began cutting away her pants. Her phone rang again while she was working. She didn't answer it.

Spencer had called her six times in the hour's times since she had seen him at the scene. She wasn't mad at him, but knew that whatever he had to say, she didn't want to hear it. Cait had screwed up; they both knew it, and him telling her again was not going to help her right now.

She had removed most of the pant leg and had washed the area as best she could when it rang again. This time it was CO Hunter. She debated answering it, but decided what the hell? In for a penny, in for a pound, as her uncle had said.

"I'm busy right now, why don't you call back tomorrow?" She winced when he started cussing at her, not so much from what he was saying, but the volume in which he was doing it. She started sewing together the bullet hole until he calmed down.

"Damn it, girl, what the fuck are you trying to prove? You gotta death wish or something? Wait for my group to get to you. From what I hear, you ain't in such good shape anyway."

"Gee, Capt., way to be encouraging. Want maybe I should go out and flag down the first bad guy I see and let him know that I can barely move, so he should go ahead and kill me now?" She finished off the stitch and knotted the thread.

Taking the little pair of scissors, she snipped the thread and then started on the back wound. She had to wipe the sweat off her face twice during the procedure; the pain was excruciating.

"How much longer you gonna be at the bus station? You must have a plan in place."

Cait stopped sewing and leaned her head back against the wall. "Martinez has two places in Columbus. I thought I'd take the bus to the middle of them and then take a cab from there. The bus I want is leaving in thirty minutes. I'm going to his house first."

"Sounds like a plan. Keep me updated and I'll pass it on to Tucker for you. You armed?"

"Not well. I have the one piece I had with me when I left the house but no extra ammo. I did have a knife, but I traded it for the money to get here. I'm hurt pretty bad, Capt. I hope I can make it."

"I have no doubt you'll see this to the end, O'Malley. I'll see what I can do about having one of Tucker's men at the station for you when you arrive. Call me when you get there and I'll tell you what I have." She hung up after he did.

Hunter was in on it. She had always wondered how Cantel and his men had known where to find her at the range, and now she knew. She looked down at the phone he had given her at the hospital when hers had been broken at the first shooting. She had never taken it apart. She was glad now that she had not taken it with her everywhere she had gone.

Rummaging through the bag again, she pulled out the small cell phone and turned it on. She finished up the wound in the back of her leg and started wrapping it tight as she dialed. After three rings, he answered.

"Did you send those folders off for me?" she asked when he answered. She hoped her uncle and she had been right about this man, but now, she had no choice.

"I hand delivered them myself just now. Fact is, I'm still in their driveway. They're all at the mother's house. Wasn't too happy to see me, 'cause I wouldn't give them anything, but I can live with it. That man, Spencer, I don't think he'll be able to shit for a month I crawled so far up his ass for what he did to you," Captain Tucker told her.

"He's entitled to his opinion. In fact, it doesn't differ that much from my own. Hunter just called. We were right. He's as deep as he can be. He knows where I am and he is supposed to call you with information on my whereabouts."

"And you gonna share with me where you are too? It would be nice to be in on some of what's going on, seeing as how it's going on in my town. You know where that little girl is, don't you, O'Malley?"

"Yes. I'm going to go to his house. It's near the Scioto River. Do you have someone you can trust to help me out? I may need a ride there."

"Yeah, me. Tell me what you need and I'll be there. By the way, do you trust me, O'Malley?"

Yes, she did. She didn't know what it was about the man, but trust had never been an issue with him. Her uncle Paddy had said the same thing about him.

"Yeah, Tucker, I do. This is what I need…"

An hour later, she was getting on a COTA and traveling to the closest stop there was to where she was going. It just happened to be the Columbus Zoo.

~~~

Spencer was still pacing. He had been doing that since he had walked in the door to his mother's home, and hadn't stopped since. He wanted to know what Devin was doing, but short of breaking the door down, he couldn't just barge into the study.

186

The cop, Tucker, the one he had met at the picnic, had shown up about two hours ago and asked to speak to Devin. Devin seemed surprised and when questioned, Tucker told them that he had no more information on the shooting than he had before and that his visit right now was personal. When Devin had come forward, Tucker simply handed him the large envelope. He then told Devin that he was doing this for a friend and that other than what the contents were, he didn't know the details. Then he left.

When the study door opened and Devin walked out, Spencer saw the look on his brother's face and knew something bad had happened. He wanted to ask, but instead, just waited for Devin to get a drink and sit down.

"You all right? You look like you've seen a ghost. Anything I can do to help you out?"

Devin looked up at him in a dazed, faraway look. "I just finalized the funeral arrangements for Patrick and Deidre O'Malley. Captain Tucker brought me the paperwork that named me the executor of their estate. Caitlynne O'Malley signed the job over to me two weeks ago."

"Why you? I'm sorry, that didn't come out right. I mean, why did she name you the one...shit, Devin, you know what I mean."

"Yes, I do. There were letters with the file—one from each of them. The letters weren't addressed to me, at least the ones from Caitlynne's aunt and uncle weren't. Theirs said that in the event they were dead, Caitlynne or the surviving other would choice an attorney to fulfill the terms of their will to the letter. Cait's was to me. Would you like to read it?"

Spencer was nodding yes before his heart told him this was a bad idea. He knew that he was going to regret this. And knowing what he knew about the O'Malley family, he knew that it would be straight forward and concise. There would be no details other than the ones needed to make the arrangements. But he found himself reaching for the envelope and opening it.

Mr. Grant,

If you are reading this letter it means that my aunt and uncle are both dead. Let me explain to you what we have done.

In the years since my father was killed and my mother committed suicide, my uncle has had arrangements made like these to ensure that his wants and needs at this time are met. My father left no will, probably thinking that my mother would finish raising me. My mother did nothing.

When I became a cop then later a detective, I knew that the chances were fairly good that I would be killed in the line of duty. I took my uncle's advice and made up my arrangements as well. I don't have a great deal to leave, but I have made changes in my will recently. You will find it enclosed too. You will need to please keep it on file as I have no one else to leave it to. Monies from our combined estate will pay you any fees you deem reasonable and customary.

You have all the bank information and copies of insurance papers you need to take care of arrangements for my aunt and uncle. Also, there are several numbers in Ireland you will need to call to have Aunt Dee's body shipped there.

Thank you for your professionalism in this very personal matter for us. My uncle and aunt liked you, regardless of how much I told them you were a pain in the ass to me.

Sincerely,
Caitlynne Alexander O'Malley

Spencer handed the envelope back to Devin and stared at the empty grate. Even making her own funeral arrangements, O'Malley had told it like it was. He looked over at Devin.

"What are the arrangements for the two of them? I'm assuming that from that letter, Dee will be going back to Ireland. What about Paddy?"

"A simple graveside service and nothing more. I had to call Tucker back and ask about that. He said that the department would want a policeman's funeral with all the pomp and circumstance, but he would relay the information to the Mayor about the change."

"Did you ask about O'Malley?" Spencer kept thinking about the things he had said to her. The way he had shaken her as if she was nothing more than the people who had taken his daughter.

"He said that it's an ongoing investigation and that he could not share that information with me. He also said to tell you to fuck off. You really pissed that guy off, didn't you?"

"You have no idea. I said some things...I didn't know he was dead, either of them, until...I told her it was her fault that Meggie had been taken. I told her that she and her family were going to pay if anything happened to Meggie. I told her to go and get my daughter. Tucker...he showed me the bodies. Paddy took nine shots trying to protect Meggie, and Dee three more. When I came up to the scene, O'Malley was sitting in the ambulance being looked at. She was...they told me later that she had been shot several times and that her wounds on her chest were bleeding again. She had a bullet go through her leg and he thought she had been shot in the head and arm as well. Christ, Devin, what am I going to do? How will I ever make this up to her?"

He sat down now. He had realized riding over here just how very much he was in love with O'Malley. And that he would do anything to get her back, but he was afraid he would never get the chance. If she lived through this, he was very much afraid that she would never want anything to do with him. And he couldn't think of one reason why she should.

~CHAPTER TWENTY~

Cait sat in the front seat of the nearly empty bus. It wasn't all that late, but it was a holiday and most places were closed. She waited until they were on the road a goodly way before she sat up and put her gun into the gut of the driver. He stiffened and would have pulled over, but she stopped him.

"Don't. I won't hurt you, but I want you to know that what I'm about to tell you is serious. I'm a homicide detective and I'm on an assignment. I'm going to show you my badge and pull my gun away. Please, give me a minute to explain."

She slowly pulled her badge from under her shirt and put it in his lap. He picked it up and glanced at it several times before he dropped it back in his lap. Cait pulled it back to her by the ball chain that held it around her neck.

"Okay, for now I'll believe you. There's a camera over my head, but from the way you're sitting and the way you pointed the gun at me, I'm assuming you know that. So, Detective, tell me a story."

"There was a shootout at my family home this morning and a little girl was kidnapped. Her family wants her back."

"News didn't mention a kid, but I saw the story. Thought I recognized the name. I'm sorry about your parents."

"Thank you. Yes, they would keep something like that under cover until she is let go. A drug lord has her and I'm going to confront him. We're being followed by a cruiser, can you see it? What I need is for you to have bus trouble. Nothing major, but something that will make you need to pull over. I'm hoping that the cop will stop and you'll be able to suddenly get it going again, but if he doesn't, then I'm getting off. I have a ride coming to get me. Can you do that?"

"Okay, sure, I can do that. How much trouble are you talking? I mean, this thing has power steering and without power, there ain't no steering." He grinned at her in the mirror.

"Whatever it takes. I leave that up to you. But you need to...I don't want you to lose your job and I promise I'll make sure that the police tell them you were aiding an officer. Are you sure you want to help out, knowing all this?"

"Yes, ma'am, I do. Just tell me when we are going to have this break down and I'll heave ho the bus for us."

Cait pulled out her clean cell and called Tucker. He answered on the first ring. He was only about three miles back and yes, he could see the car following. The officer, Samuel Weekly, was a State boy and, according to the dispatcher, he was off duty until Thursday — family issues.

"If he stops you, just drive by. I'm sure he won't confront me on the bus. They won't want that many witnesses. I'm going to call Hunter when we stop and tell him about the bus problems. I'll leave his phone on the bus and he'll note the time I start moving again and send out someone else to follow"

"You think he's going to pass you, don't you? Why would he do that? I mean, if you're standing there, why not take you out then?"

"With the bus trouble, he'll know I'm being delayed. They can switch out the person following without raising suspicion. And with this unexpected extra time, they'll think they have more time to ready for me and hopefully get a little more lax."

"When this is over, I want you to come work for me. I need someone like you on my team. You're a hell of a good detective."

She hung up and looked out the window. If things went the way she thought they would, she would not be working for anyone anymore.

Carl Reese, the bus driver, was perfect in his role as flustered driver. He had started cussing the moment she told him now and tapping the breaks like the bus was lurching. He turned off the engine and struggled to get the heavy, unyielding thing to the side of the road. The cruiser drove by. He didn't even slow down, but drove by as if he hadn't seen them.

Carl got out and raised the hood up. Cait slipped out the open door, leaving behind the cell phone and a bloody stain on the seat. She hadn't meant to leave the latter, but there was no help for it.

Captain Tucker drove up beside them and got out. While he was talking to the driver, Cait slipped into the back seat of the car and lay down. She was hurting and tried to keep her leg off the seat so that she wouldn't leave a stain, but she didn't have the strength. A minute or two later, Tucker got into the car and merged into traffic toward the mansion in Delaware.

"Janet? O'Malley, this is my sister-in-law, Janet Tucker. She's going to have a look at your wounds. She's a nurse at OSU. Janet, this is the detective I was telling you about." Tucker looked at her through the rearview mirror as Janet crawled to the middle bench seat to tend her.

"Hi, I've got you some extra clothes and Don brought you an extra vest too. I'm going to have a...sheesh, lady you sew these yourself? Pretty good, but I can make them tighter. I also have some fluids I want you to push, mostly juice. Don said you were bleeding and might need something. I have some food for you too. It's just light stuff, but I want you to eat as much as you can before we get there."

Cait was too weak to argue. The pain radiating from her leg was outdistancing the pain in her head by leaps and bounds. She was still very dizzy and every time she sat up, the car tilted in ways that made her belly jump. Tucker starting talking to her as Janet worked.

"I talked to your lawyer again since I talked to you last. He told me about your uncle's plans to have only a graveside service. I don't suppose it's possible for you to go against his wishes on that? He died doing a cop's job; he deserves a policeman's funeral."

"He made those arrangements after he retired. I'm sure he never thought he would be in...that he would go like he did. As far as changing them, I'm not sure what his will says. But by giving Mr. Grant POA, he can pretty much do what he wants. You should tell him your thoughts and let him decide."

She couldn't tell Tucker that she was going to be long gone before Uncle Paddy's funeral. If she made it through tonight, she was going to go to Ireland to bury her aunt before she did anything else. Every time she closed her eyes, she could still see his body lying there and the look of shock in her aunt's eyes. Neither of them deserved this and it broke her heart that she had caused so much heartache.

"I'll do that. Paddy was a good man and I don't think I've ever met a man more proud of anyone as he was of you. The day you got your gold shield, he came into the squad room with pictures and showed them to everybody. I think I probably saw them more than anyone; he liked to hang out in my office all the time. Then when you got shot, I thought the man had aged ten years in the few hours it took us to make arrangements to get him to you."

"What do you mean? He didn't drive? I thought he and Aunt Dee drove over themselves. I don't remember much from the first, but I thought his car was already there."

"Nah, none of us wanted to think about him driving on his own and your aunt Dee was falling apart. Two of us drove them over in that car of his and then we drove back. He sobbed the whole way over telling us how you were an O'Malley and that you'd better not die."

"You were with him. I didn't know. He never...when he brought me here he said that he had good friends and that he didn't know what he'd do without them. I didn't know what he meant; I was in so much pain."

"I was serious about you coming to work for me. I need good detectives and you are top notch. When this is all over—"

"Captain Tucker, when this is all over I'm going to be considered a snitch and we both know how well those kinds of cops do. I'm going into this with seven deaths on my hands, not including the three in Chicago. After today, there will be at least one more. If I'm not up on murder charges, I'm going to be before the board for a long time before they get this sorted out."

Neither of them said anything as the road flew by, both trapped in their own misgivings about what was about to happen. Cait figured she was going to be killed, either by the men in the house or by the cops when she came out. Killing a cop never went over well.

When they were on the street leading up to the house near the river, Cait got out and down to the beach front. She was going to walk to the house from this end using the private property as a cover. It was dark now and would be full dark when she got inside the house. Tucker was taking Janet to a hotel to wait for them.

~~~

Spencer was sitting at the table with his family, playing with his food, when the house phone rang at nearly nine o'clock. There had been so many calls, people wanting to know if they had heard anything, the police asking if they had heard from Cait. It had been nearly ten hours since the attack on the O'Malley home and there was still no news about Meggie or Cait. When Jamie came in the dining room from the kitchen and said the phone was for him, Spencer didn't know how to react. He went to the kitchen to see what bad news there was now.

"Doctor Grant? This is Captain Tucker. I wanted you to know that I've just left Detective O'Malley. We are closer to getting your daughter back. A lot of things could go wrong, but I think we have the element of surprise on our side."

"Is O'Malley all right? I know you don't think I have a right to ask, but I need to know. I...I'm in love with her and I...I can't tell you how much I hate myself right now."

"You're right; you don't have a right to ask. But I'll tell you anyway. She has fourteen stitches in her leg, ten of which she put there herself. A head wound she wouldn't let anyone dress. I don't know about the bleeding in her chest, she was pretty adamant about letting no one tend to that, but she was moving on her own when I saw her last. If she lives through this, she will need rest and support. I don't believe you're the man for the job, but Janet seems to think you might be. I'll call you when I know more. Your house is being watched, by the way, and not by my men. Don't leave to go near the zoo without taking precautions. Could get someone killed that way. Understand? And don't use your cell; my men are watching that one."

"Yes, I understand. Thank you. Thank you very much." Spencer turned around and his entire family was standing in the doorway just inside the kitchen.

"Well, where are we going? He did tell you where she was, didn't he? And if you think you're going without us then you aren't near as smart as I thought you were," his mother said when no one else said anything.

"Yes, he did, but you can't go with me. Wait! Listen, he said that I had to take precautions, that the house was being watched by Martinez's men. He also told me not to use my cell phone, that his people were monitoring it. I have to go to Delaware, near the zoo. I'm assuming that once I get there, I'll know where to go."

"I'll drive. Your car is known all over the place and mine isn't here. David called this morning and told me to pick it up and with everything going on, I forgot about it. Now we need a distraction. Honey, anything come to mind?" Dan winked at his wife and Spencer flushed.

Dan was his step-father and he was the most reserved man he knew. When he winked at their mother like that, Spence couldn't help but remember the time he had walked in on them getting...frisky, his mother had called it, on the kitchen table.

The fire truck showed up seven minutes later. His mother had set the kitchen on fire with the promise that Spencer would pay for all the remodeling for her sacrifice. Spencer wasn't sure what kind of sacrifice she had been making; his mother never cooked when someone else could and if there was not anyone to cook for her, ordering in or going out was just as good. He was still chuckling about it when he and Dan slipped into Dan's car at the garage where it had been getting serviced.

"Your mom, she's something else, isn't she? You don't worry about the kitchen job. It'll be my pleasure to set it to rights. I know this is very serious business and I know that that girl will get Meggie back for you, but I gotta tell you, son, I've never enjoyed watching a kitchen burn up so much in my life."

~CHAPTER TWENTY-ONE~

Cait only encountered one dog at one of the neighbors' as she moved along the back. He had been so excited to have someone talk to him; he had nearly knocked her down in his effort to let Cait pet him. She thought for sure he was going to have serious back problems with the way he had wiggled.

The house was lit up like they had stock in the power company. Cait had a few problems getting to the house. There had been three guards and she took care of them quietly. And from them, she picked up another Glock, this one with a modified silencer on it.

The first man had startled her. He had worn his uniform that showed he was with Chicago PD. At first she thought he was there to help her and when he drew his gun and shot at her, she instinctively fired back and killed him. The next one she encountered was dressed in black, but was no less of a cop. Even his vest said "police" on it and she knew him from another shift. When he drew his weapon and leered at her, she shot him as well. The last, a big guy, had come up behind her when she was searching the second vic.

He hit her with his body and she went tumbling head over ass. When she staggered to her feet, he ran at her and caught her in her belly with his shoulder, knocking her down again. Cait was dizzy now and she knew she was bleeding again. That was when Tucker decided to check in.

"What's happening? I can hear you, but I don't have the slightest—"

Tucker had borrowed his sister's head set for her phone and had Cait use her own device. He called her phone and made sure there was a good connection before she had ventured off. Cait was impressed. She had thought she was going to be on her own.

"Busy. Shut up," she snapped when her assailant hit her in the face with his fist. She could not take much more in the way of abuse, she realized, and knew that she had to do something quick.

"Don't tell me to shut up. I want to know what the fuck is going on. Are you in trouble?" At this point, Cait pulled out the modified Glock and shot the man drawing back his fist to hit her again.

"I have to hang up now. I'll call—"

"You will not. I want to know what the hell you've been doing or I'm coming in," Tucker screamed in her ear.

"Suit yourself." She leaned over and started retching.

The truth of the matter was, she probably could have done it a lot quieter, but Tucker had pissed her off and she added a few more moans and sound effects than was really necessary. Her head was spinning when she knew she had sicked up everything, so she lay down.

"Christ! A little warning next time would not have hurt you one bit. Are you okay, kid? I think you should come back and let's wait on the back-up."

"No, I'm not...Tucker, I need a favor. When this is over, I mean." She closed her eyes, but that only made her head pound more. She was in serious pain, first from earlier and now from the beating. Throwing up had not helped all that much either.

"What is it before I agree? I've not known you long, but I know enough about you to know that you don't ask for help much." She heard him chuckle, but she was too hurt to appreciate it.

"The last envelope, make sure that the instructions are followed. They aren't just for my death, but arrangements for me today. I don't care if you give Uncle...my uncle Paddy a policeman's honor, but mine...just promise you'll follow the instructions. All right?"

"Caitlynne, don't do this. You're going to get that little girl, the doc is going to see the error of his ways, and you'll come work for me. All is good, you'll see."

She didn't answer him, but stood up and when the ground settled back down, she started moving across the lawn again. Hurting in places she didn't know she had, she wondered how she was going to get Meggie out once she found her.

Moving along the perimeter, she made her way up to the house and next to the back door. She had seen movement in one of the lower rooms, but the head

203

injury was making it hard for her to make out just who they were.

"I'm here. I can see three people in what looks like a study. There is a desk and shelves," Cait whispered in the headset.

"How many people have you seen so far? There were what, three you've killed and now the three in the house? Not that I doubt your ability to do what you set out, but I still have to explain."

Cait stopped progress in picking the lock on the door. "I thought you said that I needed to get in and get out. Can't very well do that if I have to keep a body count, now can I? Back off, Tucker. I'm not killing anyone that hasn't tried to kill me. Use of Force Continuum—I understand the rules."

She did too. Never use more force than necessary. When as adversary uses his fists, one couldn't very well pull out your gun and shoot him. Tempting as it was, it wasn't fair or legal.

The lock snapped open with a little click and she eased the door open. She could smell that she had entered the kitchen and quickly shut the door behind her when she realized the room was empty. There was another door across from her and a quick look showed it to be a large pantry. Moving toward the far door, she found another door that led to a small half bath. There was a huge block on the butcher block that held an assortment of knives. She took two of the thinner bladed ones and stuck them into her shirt sleeve, blades down. She drew her gun out again and went to the only door left.

This one opened into a dining room. The room had a large oval table with a dozen chairs around it. The chandelier was off, but there were several small battery operated candle in the six windows around the dark room. Cait could see the wall sized hutch filled with dishes and another one across from it that was filled with glasses. Moving to the open doorway, she could hear voices down the hall.

"I'm moving deeper into the house. If I don't answer right away, don't freak out on me again. I can hear people talking down the hall. I think it was the study I saw from outside," she whispered to Captain Tucker, and smiled when he whispered back. No one could hear him, but he still did it.

"I don't freak out, but all right. Heads up, the back-ups are here. Men I trust. I'll hold back until you have the little girl safe, then we'll move in."

She kept to the shadows and was alert to anyone else who might be in the house. She was at the bottom of a staircase and looked up to see that it, like the rest of the house, was lit up. She could only see three doors and all but one was opened. And outside of it stood an armed man dressed in a dark suit.

She got as close to the study as she could and listened to see if she could hear what was going on and if she recognized anyone. There were three different voices and the one doing the most talking right then was Martinez.

"I don't care what you think. I'm the one footing the bills and you'll do it my way. I want that girl killed tonight. It shouldn't be any problem to slip into her hospital room and do whatever necessary to take her out of the picture. Christ! She has been hounding me since that partner of hers fucked up. I want her dead." The accompanying slam of something hard against wood made her laugh to herself.

At first, she thought he was talking about Meggie. But he had only just met her, so Cait realized it was her. She didn't know what he was talking about until Tucker whispered.

"I can hear him. I'm assuming that's Martinez. Um, didn't know it until just now, but you are apparently in the hospital in critical condition. The bus driver, a good citizen, called an ambulance when he had bus problems. Your phone was taken back to OSU. You should make a full recovery, though. Good to know. What sort of flowers should I get you?" Her low growl made him chuckle.

She wondered how he had "just found out," but decided it really didn't matter right now.

"I got a man going there now. He'll take care of her. What about the girls? There is a ship sitting in New York with twenty-three prostitutes waiting to be put to work and nearly a ton of coke. I have to contact my guys up North to get it moved. They don't like having something that huge sitting in the harbor." Cait closed her eyes and leaned back against the wall for support.

She knew that her old boss Hunter was involved with Martinez, she just hadn't known how deep. Tucker speaking again startled her.

"Cait, I'm recording this. Can you tell me who that was who just spoke? If not, then you'll have to tell me later."

"Hunter," she whispered. "Captain David Hunter, of the Chicago Police Department. I have to go dark side for a few minutes. I'm leaving you here to listen in. Don't do anything stupid." She took the blue tooth off her ear and set it on the table next to the doorway. Tucker was talking and she had a good idea what he was saying, but she needed to see if she could find Meggie.

Moving past the dining room again, she found what looked like might have been an entertainment room. This room, like the kitchen, was dark and had no one inside. She crossed the room to another and found what she needed. A back set of stairs.

Quietly, she moved up them, keeping to the sides in case they gave away her position with a creak. She was nearly to the top when someone came out of one of the rooms and stopped and turned to the guard. She stepped back down until she could see over the stairs and the person talking to the guard.

"She won't eat. And I can't get her to say a damned word. Why the hell he brought her here is beyond me. I hate kids, especially stupid ones that don't listen. Well, if she won't eat then she'll fucking go hungry."

Cait watched the woman move down the opposite set of stairs with a tray in her hands. The guard watched her and Cait slipped up the stairs and into the room the other woman had just left. Cait had just shut the door behind her when Meggie grabbed her leg.

"Oh baby! I'm so sorry. You can't...let me look at you. Did they hurt you?" Cait touched Meggie and realized that someone had hit her. Probably the woman, but Meggie was upset enough without asking her to relive what had to be a painful hit.

Her little face was bruised badly and there was a small cut on her lip. She knew that this was all her fault. If she had not said she would watch over Meggie then she would be safe with her father right now.

"I want my daddy. Can you take me to him? Please, O'Malley, take me home. I don't like it here," Meggie told her.

"Me either. Yeah, we'll go, but you have to do what I tell you. There are people in the house with guns and I don't want you to get hurt anymore. When I tell you to move, you have to move."

Meggie nodded and hugged Cait again. Pain reverberated through her body from the contact, but she needed the hug as much as Meggie did.

Cait opened the door slightly and looked out to where the guard had been standing when she had gone into the bedroom. He wasn't there, but that didn't mean he was not close. She had Meggie stay in the room as she went out into the hall.

He slammed the door into her back as she was stepping through the opening. The impact knocked her down and she skidded on the carpet, burning her arms and smearing blood onto the cream-colored carpet. When he leaned over her to pick her up, she brought her leg up and kicked him hard in the balls. It took a full second before the pain registered on his face. When he dropped forward and onto her, she used the momentum to flip him back off of her. She misjudged how close she was to the stairs and he went over the railing. Before he hit the floor below, Cait was up and rushing toward Meggie.

Cait had to hide her because any minute they were all going to be coming up the stairs, guns drawn. Meggie was standing right where Cait had left her. Grabbing her hand, she tugged her out into the hall and looked around. Taking her to the grandfather clock that stood along the outside wall, Cait opened the door and nearly sobbed in relief.

Sounds were coming from downstairs now and she dropped in front of Meggie. Cait was thinking of the best way to make her understand how important it was that she remain here until she or her daddy came for her when Meggie nodded and crawled into the space.

It was tight and once the door was closed, it would be dark. Thinking quickly, Cait pulled out her keys and gave them to Meggie. There was a small key light on it and she showed it to Meggie. Reaching into her front pocket again, she pulled out the picture of Meggie and her daddy that Devin had given her. Kissing the picture, Cait handed it to her. Smiling huge, Meggie nodded and pulled the door closed.

Cait ran to the window and opened it just as three men appeared from the front steps and two at the back. One fired at her head and she stopped. Another grabbed her by her vest and threw her to the floor while another went to the window and looked out.

"You know, I'm fucking sick and tired of being thrown around by you fucks. Have you ever thought to ask me to—" The guy who had thrown her to the floor kicked her in the ribs and she doubled up in pain.

She pulled out the gun at her waist and fired three times.

The three men closest to her dropped. Cait turned to fire onto the other two when her gun was kicked from her hand. She knew that she was dead, but the familiar voice from the stairwell stopped all movement.

"Kill her and I'll make you suffer in ways you cannot fathom. Ah, Caitlynne O'Malley, I presume? I've heard so many...shall we say, lovely things about you. Quite impressive, you've managed to get past my guard and take out four of my men before we could apprehend you. Sad, don't you think?" Anthony Martinez pulled out his gun and shot the remaining two men.

~Chapter Twenty-Two~

Spencer listened to the noises coming through the phone. The clarity was amazing and sickening at the same time. He could hear the men talking about the ship in the harbor and what they planned to do with the young girls on it. The coke, they planned to disperse all over the Eastern part of the United States.

"Why can't we hear O'Malley anymore? I know you said she said she was going dark side, but I guess I'm not sure what that means exactly," he asked the cop.

"It means that I'm going to beat that girl's ass when I see her next time. She is not saying anything because she's not carrying the only way of communication we have. I can understand why she did it, but I don't have to be happy about it."

When Spencer and Dan had pulled up in front of the Donald Tucker's car, he had them open their hood and if anyone came by they would think they were working on a broken down car. It seemed like a good idea at the time, but now there were several cars around them, all police in their personal cars. Donald had told him that just down the road there were

211

several other cruisers and an ambulance waiting for word from Cait to come running.

The captain had been ranting for the past forty minutes about how much he was going to enjoy writing O'Malley up and then he was going to put her on desk duty for an entire year. He said it would take that long for him to calm down enough to let her go out in the public again.

"Did she say she was going to work for you then? I thought she was planning to go back to her home after this." Spencer knew as soon as the words were out of his mouth he had set the man off again. If it wasn't so serious, Spencer might have enjoyed goading him into another rant.

"She damned well will be working for me. I need my payback. To think that I had my sister — "

They all froze when the crash happened. It was loud and very close to where the speaker was. Tucker had picked up the mike to call in the troops when they heard the shouting. It was not Cait; that was all the three men could conjecture. They waited for what seemed like an eternity for something to happen. The gun shots were not what they had hoped for.

~~~

Martinez flipped his gun at Cait to indicate that she should precede him down the stairs. Cait wasn't sure she wanted the man behind her, but figured if he wanted her dead; he would have killed her or let one of his men do it. She didn't look at the clock, hoping that Meggie stayed where she was for a little while longer.

About halfway down the stairs, she saw that the table in the middle of the hall had been crushed from the man she had thrown over the railing. Glancing at the other table, she was glad to see that the little receiver she had put there had not been disturbed. When she was close enough, she tripped and landed against the table. She grabbed up the little thing and attached it to the front of her jeans pocket.

"In there." Martinez pointed to the room she'd heard them in earlier. And if you try anything stupid, or stupider I should say, I will shoot you. David, call one of those idiots in the yard and tell them to be on the lookout for a little girl. Tell them if anyone needs to shoot her, so be it."

"I've been trying to raise them since you went upstairs," Hunter said to them as he laid down the two-way. "No one is answering. You think there's something wrong with their reception?" Cait giggled and earned a hard slap in the back of the head from Martinez.

"How many of his men did you take out, Caitlynne? And who is helping you? Should I be worried that someone is going to come crashing through the door now that the kid is gone?"

"Three idiots and the two dogs. And you really should be worried, Martinez. I'm going to kill you both before I leave here." Cait hit the floor when she was kicked in the ribs again.

"You really think I'm afraid of you? I mean, look at you. You look like someone has beaten the shit out of you several times already and you're about ten minutes from your own death. And I do believe your hand is broken. Carl kicked you pretty good and if I'm not mistaken, that was your shooting hand. You're lying here on my floor bleeding to death and no one gives two shits if you live or die. You're responsible for the death of your entire family and you're going to die all alone."

Cait sat up on her hand and knees and took a couple of breaths. She knew that at least two of her ribs were broken and he was probably right about her hand. A couple of her fingers were bent at an odd angle and it was swelling. Blood was dripping from her nose onto the carpet beneath her and probably her lip as well. Running her tongue over her teeth, she realized that at some point they had loosened and she had bit her tongue. Moaning, she moved to her knees and looked up at the two men. She hoped that Tucker got all the information he needed because she was not going to make it much longer.

Raising her hand to her face, she scrubbed the blood from her forehead and smiled at them. Anthony had a gun, but it was hanging loosely in his hand. Hunter had never taken his from his holster. She swayed slightly and grabbed for the floor again. Taking another short breath, she pulled the Glock that she had taken from the guy in the yard and fired at Martinez first.

He moved when the gun came up and she hit him in the throat, but he dropped the gun when he grabbed for his neck. The next shot hit Hunter in the forehead. He dropped back hard against Martinez and both landed on the floor. Cait knew that she didn't have much time, her body was starting to want to move less

SPENCER

and less, and she painfully stood up and staggered to the desk that they had fallen behind.

Martinez was staring up at her and his arms lay limply out from his body. Moving toward the two men, she kicked the weapon away that he had used to kill the men upstairs and then she opened Hunter's jacket and tossed his gun a foot or so away.

She had had enough and fell back on her ass and leaned against the chair as Martinez died. She nearly closed her eyes when she remembered Tucker and Meggie, and she pulled the headset from her pants and put it into her ear.

"Tucker? You there?" She closed her eyes; the room spinning was making her sick again. She knew that she had nothing left to sick up, but she still felt like she needed to.

"Caitlynne? Christ, where are you? We're coming in and I don't want to hear another word—"

"Please, listen. Dead, they're all dead. Meggie is in the clock at the top of the...there is a clock up there and I put Meggie...Tucker? Are you there?" She was drifting out and she knew that she was barely hanging on to consciousness. She knew she was not dying, not yet at any rate, but her body was telling her "enough already, let's rest a minute."

"Meggie is in the clock. Yeah, we're coming. Hang on, help is on the way. Caitlynne, do you hear me?"

"You promised. Remember? I...don't have...tell Spen...Doctor Grant that I...her lip is hurt. I'm sorry." Closing her eyes this time, she saw her uncle Paddy. "Hi there. Have you come to get me?" She wanted to reach for him, but nothing worked anymore. But when

215

he touched her cheek, everything faded out and she let it.

~CHAPTER TWENTY-THREE~

Spencer stood next to the cruiser and paced. They had told him he could go and get Meggie as soon as they cleared that there were no more men inside. Tucker had left him a radio so that he could hear when the all clear was given. He was also supposed to let him know if Cait was all right.

"Doctor Grant? It's clear. There are a set of stairs right as you come in. At the top is a clock. None of my men have gone near it, only to guard it until you get here. Go."

Spencer did not have to be told twice. Taking off at a run, he went up the stairs three at a time and stopped in front of the clock. There was a bullet hole in the glass where the chime had been. His heart skipped several beats as he dropped to his knees in front of the clock and slowly reached for the door.

When he opened it slowly, Meggie was resting her head against the back of it, playing with a set of keys and holding a small piece of paper. When she looked over, blinking rapidly from the unexpected light, she tumbled out and fell on top of him, kissing and hugging him. Spencer felt the tears streaming down his face and didn't care who saw them. He had his baby girl.

Her hands were between them and she struggled against him to get them out. He didn't want to let her go, not even for this, but also needed to hear what she had to say. He had to slow her down twice, but he got what she wanted. He picked her up and they descended the stairs to where the gurney was being taken.

"Doctor Grant, you don't want to take the little girl in there. It's not a sight I want to remember, much less subject to a kid. Life flight is on their way. They're going to take her to OSU and there is a team there waiting for her. The medic has called it in. I'll take you in the car. She'll probably be in surgery by the time we get there."

"I want to go with her. Please, I want to be with her. I won't get in the—" Spencer stopped when Captain Tucker continued to shake his head.

"They have to have all the room in that thing to be able to move around. She is in critical but stable condition. Why don't you take Meggie in the other room? There is another cop in there who wants to ask her some questions and you could help out in translating for her. I need as much information as I can get from her, Spence. And I swear to you, O'Malley is in the best hands."

Spencer knew that he was right, but he needed to see her. He handed Meggie to him, told her to wait, and he walked into the study. All the blood nearly had him turning around, but he wanted to see Cait for himself.

The first things he saw were the medics and an empty gurney. There was a person using a camera and another with a video camera filming all around the room. He had seen the same kind of set up when he had been upstairs and didn't realize that there were so many people involved in a crime scene.

One of the men moved over slightly and he saw her. Christ, she was a mess. Even from where he stood he knew that she had not only taken a beating, but she had been shot as well. The left side of her face, all he could really see from where he stood, was puffy and bloody. He could just make out her lower lip; it was nearly touching her chin it was so badly beaten. Blood matted her hair and her arm. One of the medics had put something like a board on her hand and was gently wrapping the splint with some gauze. They had cut her pant leg open and there was a rapidly reddening pad there as well. When she started to shake, tremble like her body was chilled, the men laid her down on the floor and covered her with a blanket. They never stopped talking to her, he realized. They told her everything they were doing to her and when they were going to touch her. The older man kept telling her to hang on, she would be safe soon.

Spencer walked back out into the hall and Meggie reached up to be held. He took her and realized that if he didn't sit down soon, he was going to fall. Donald must have sensed how close he was and suddenly, there was a chair under him. It took Spencer several seconds to realize that he was talking to him.

"...broken, but the medic said it's clean. Five ribs are either broken or bruised, but her lungs are fine.

Her face looks bad, but the only thing broken is her nose and she'll need stitches over both eyes and her lip. There's a cut along her jaw, but he doesn't want to speculate on where it came from and can't tell me what is going to happen to it until they figure it out. The GSW in her leg is from this morning and she has lost a great deal of blood, but nothing that she won't be able to naturally replace. They've tried to start and IV, but because of the extensive damage done to her arms, they can't find a good vein."

"Damage? That doesn't sound good. What happened to them? And when will she be awake?"

"Damage might have been the wrong word to use. I should have said hurt. She looks like she slid across the carpet and burnt them that way, then the broken hand, and her shoulder is dislocated like I said."

"Captain, life flight ETA is two minutes. They want us to take her out into the yard. Officer Brown has circled the cars to make a landing pad and they said they can see it. They're ready in here," an officer said from the study door.

Spencer stood when Donald did. He knew he had to call his family. They would be anxious to hear that Meggie was safe and that Cait was on her way to the hospital. He pulled out his cell phone on the way out of the house.

When his mother answered the phone, all Spencer could do was sob. He could not say a word. She started crying too. He had to tell her and working around the huge knot in his throat, he said it all.

"I have her. I have them both." He heard her tell someone with her and he had to pull the phone from his ear; the shouts were loud and immediate. He could hear his brother Nicky whistle and yelling, "hell yeah!"

"And Caitlynne, how is she? Please, Spencer, please let her be all right," his mom begged.

"They're taking her by life flight to OSU as a precautionary measure. I'm going to go over in a cruiser. Could you...will one of you come and bring Meggie something to change into and something to eat? She said she didn't have anything all day."

"Of course. I'll meet you there. Tell Dan I love him. I love you too, son. She'll pull through, you'll see. Caitlynne is made of good stock."

He got off the phone a few minutes later and told Meggie what was going on. She had already told him she was staying with him, that she had missed him. He was fine with that; he had missed her too.

Sitting in the cruiser waiting for Donald to finish up enough where he could leave, Spencer thought about the woman who, as they drove along the highway, speeding to her, was being prepped for surgery in the air. She had saved his little girl for him, saved her at great physical harm to herself not once, not even twice, but several times. And he wondered if she would ever forgive him.

He thought about how he had yelled at her, screamed at her about her not watching and keeping his daughter safe. He knew that Cait would have done more, had done more than anyone he knew to save her. Had it have been anyone else, he was sure they would not have survived even half of what she had.

The ride to the hospital took them forty minutes. The hospital had called while in route and said that

Detective O'Malley had made the flight without incident and they were taking her to the surgery room right now. Spencer got a call from his mother when she pulled into a parking space in the garage and she would meet him on the second floor. Meggie had fallen asleep, for which Spencer was grateful. She looked exhausted.

The surgeries took almost two hours. They were able to repair her hand, but she would have problems with it for some time and would need physical therapy as it started to heal. Her leg was stitched up again and they had put a removable cast on it to keep it steady as it healed. Cait's chest wounds were bruised, but the vest she had had on both times she had been shot had kept them intact. A doctor had stitched up her face; the two cuts over her eyes had required seven and nine stitches respectively and her lip another ten. Her ribs had not hit her lungs and they would need to heal on their own over the next several weeks.

Spencer now sat in an uncomfortable chair in Cait's room, waiting for her to be transferred. The doctor was making arrangements to have a private room set up for them when she got out of recovery. Spencer smiled when he thought about Doctor Hamilton and his frustration at Spencer when he had first came out to talk to them.

"Are you with the officer? Her family?"

"She's a detective and, yes, we're with her. Did she make it all right? She's sort of stubborn and I think she'd live just to spite me," Spencer said. He was babbling, but he was suddenly tired and he wanted to lie down next to her.

"I can't give you any information unless you're her family. You understand, don't you? Privacy and all. So...are you her family?"

"I don't think she has any family left. You see, they were killed this morning in a shootout that resulted in my daughter being taken. Cait saved her and I—"

"Yeah, doc, this is her husband. That's their little girl. He's a little stressed out, as you can imagine. Poor guy, yeah, these people have been through a lot," Tucker said. When Spencer started to correct him, the doctor put his hand up and glared at Spencer. He shut up.

The doctor shook his head and sat down with them. He nodded when Captain Tucker sat down too.

"And I suppose you're what, the long lost uncle? Whatever. Detective...Grant is going to be fine. She will need a lot of physical therapy and quite a bit of rest. I would suggest that you set up an in-house nurse to stay with her. She should be ready to go home in a week."

"A week? Are you sure? She looked really bad when I saw her before she went into surgery. I'm sorry; doc, but I'd like a second opinion. My brother, Damon Grant, would you care if he looked her over? I love this woman and I don't...she can't be, that is to say..."

"Yes, of course. I'm familiar with Damon. Most of her wounds were deep bruises. Yes, her leg and her hand are going to be the most painful, but the only thing we can do for her here is med her. She'll heal much faster at home surrounded by her family.

Sometimes family...O'Malley? You mean she's Paddy O'Malley's niece? Hell!"

"What is it? What's wrong? You remembered something?" Spencer stood up, ready to go and save her.

"No, no nothing like that. A few weeks ago she was a patient here and Oscar Patterson, a doctor here, saw her. I guess she ripped into him so bad that he went to the Hospital head. When Montgomery came down to question her about it, your wife ripped into him too. Threatened to file discrimination charges against him and the hospital if Montgomery didn't make him retire or apologize, and right quick too. He retired Friday. Left so quick his desk still has stuff in the drawers—the pull out sort, not the wearing sort. You don't worry about your wife, Mr. Grant. There isn't a person in this hospital that wouldn't fall over backwards for her. Damn, wish I had been here that day. I heard that Patterson sputtered all the way back to his office."

Spencer smiled again. The fact that she had taken on a doctor did not surprise him, not in the least bit. She was a fighter. He turned toward the door when it opened and Donald came in with an officer Spencer had never seen before.

"Can I have a word with you? Out here in the hall?" Spencer frowned, but went into the hall with him. He was confused when the officer came out with him.

"She made me promise. I'm sorry, but this is the first opportunity I've had to look at the envelope she gave me. Cait has requested that I put a guard on her door until I can have her moved to another facility."

"What do you mean moved? Moved where? I'm going to go back in there and wait for her. I'd like to see you stop me." His heart was pounding; she was locking him out.

"I'm sorry, Spencer, but she gave me this in the event of anything happening to her and what I was to do. She gave it to me a few days ago. All officers have these arrangements. Mostly it's to save the family from having to make hard decisions. She won't be...she's already gone, left the hospital."

Spencer leaned heavily against the wall. She was gone? How? She was still in recovery. She was... He looked at Tucker.

"You have to tell me where she is. I love her and I can't...I won't live without her. Where is she, Donald?"

"I'm sorry."

~CHAPTER TWENTY-FOUR~

Cait woke up to the sound of squeaky steps. She knew she was in a hospital; the issue was, where at? She could not tell from the equipment in the room. It looked like any other hospital room she had been in. The small ball chain attached to her gown took some maneuvering, but she was finally able to get it between her fingers and pull it.

"Yes, Miss O'Malley, what can I do for you?" the voice asked and was still no help to Cait.

"I was wondering if...could you come in here, please? I want to ask you some things, please?" After she agreed, Cait waited. She started thinking how to ask where she was without sounding like she was off her rocker when the woman walked in.

"How long have I been here, please? I know that I was hurt on Sunday, but I don't remember much after that."

"You arrived here on Monday afternoon and its Wednesday afternoon. I believe they transported you from the airport to here around shift change, so that'd be around three. We've never had an American transported here before; usually Americans want to leave. Is there anything else? The doctor said you could have some light foods, maybe some broth, and we can see how that goes?"

Cait didn't really want anything to eat, but she nodded and the nurse left. Ireland. She was in Ireland just like she had asked Captain Tucker to send her. She lay back on the bed.

If he managed this, then she knew that the rest had also been taken care of. Closing her eyes, she remembered her Uncle Paddy and how she had gotten him killed, her Aunt Dee too. Meggie had been hurt and her father...Spencer hated her for it. Cait's heart ached, wishing not for the first time that she had just died the night that Toby and his gang had tried to kill her.

When the nurse, Nurse Kiley, came back in thirty minutes later, she had a large tray. Cait knew that she needed to eat to regain her strength, but the smell made her a little queasy. Before she could ask if she had a message, Kiley handed her a large envelope.

"We were told to give this to you when you first woke up. I know that your eye is still very swollen, so if you need me to read it to you, it would be my pleasure."

Cait shook her head. Her eyesight was a little off, but she didn't want to share the news in the envelope with anyone.

After she left, Cait opened the envelope with shaky hands and pulled out the neatly typed note. She was terrified at what it might contain, but couldn't bring herself to not read it. Adjusting the letter back and forth in front of her to get the best angle for her eyes, she began to read.

"O'Malley,

This is a mistake. You and I both know it, but I've done what you've asked. There are no charges being brought against you, in neither the shootout at the mansion nor at the house. You're aunt Dee's body has been shipped to Ireland and I'm arranging a full honor funeral for your uncle – the city is picking up the tab in gratitude for what you all did.

Meggie is fine, but her father is going to be pissed. I won't tell him anything when I tell him you're gone, but as I've said, this is a mistake.

Live your life to the fullest,

Donald"

Tears streamed down her face. This was not a mistake no matter what Donald thought. And Spencer was only going to be pissed because he could not carry through on his threat to harm her because she hadn't protected Meggie enough. This was the best course of action, not only for them, but for herself.

The nurse came in sometime later to take the tray away and she mumbled something about Caitlynne not eating enough, but didn't offer to bring something else. Cait was hurting, bleeding in a place where her heart was, and she didn't care if she ever ate again.

The doctor came in the next morning and examined her. She told him that she was ready to go home and he disagreed. Cait knew he was probably right, but that did not stop her from threatening him with just leaving.

"You stay two more days and I'll let you go. Provided no infections and you have no fever. I don't want you back in here with an infection on top of everything else. You look as if whoever you're hiding from beat you well enough and I can understand you being afraid, but honey, I won't let anyone near you. You just rest and get well."

She let him think that was why she was here. There was no point in telling him that she was only hiding from herself. She told him that in two days she was going anyway and he just laughed at her.

The next two days went by slowly for her. She watched television and stared out the window. It was a beautiful view, the heather in full bloom and the trees swaying gently. She could see several mountain ranges beyond where she was and when she had gotten up the few times, she could see the horses in the paddock beyond.

She was released without much in the way of restrictions, other than to move slowly and rest a great deal. The doctor wanted to set up physical therapy for her, but she told him that she wanted to go to her aunt's home and rest and forget for a few days first. He kindly told her that she didn't want to wait too long, that she needed to get her leg loosened up again. Smiling back, she promised she would not.

The ride to the house was torturous and long. It really had only taken fifty minutes, but it seemed much longer. The driver, she swore, had hit every bump, every rock, and every single rut in every rode they used. By the time he had helped her up the stairs to the house, she was in near tears from the pain. She went inside and fell into the bed after taking a pain pill.

It was dark when she woke up. She had only been to this house three other times over the years, but could remember every nook and cranny in the place. Turning on a few lamps, she lit a fire in the huge gas powered fireplace and sat on one of the chairs. She had contacted the caretaker on Thursday and had asked that the house be ready for today and that some food, mostly easy to cook things, be delivered. Looking around the room, she knew that her wishes had been seen to.

She loved this house, a cottage really. There were only four rooms counting the bath. Several years ago, her aunt had had one of the bedrooms changed into a bathroom and indoor plumbing put in. The bathroom was huge.

The room had not been cut down when the bath was installed, but had used all the space for comfort. The outer wall, the one that faced the back of the house, was a bank of windows that reached from floor to ceiling. Shutters covered the lower half of them to allow the morning sun to shine through the upper half. The next outer wall held the white stone double sink and counter that filled the entire wall. There were drawers under it that Aunt Dee had kept her under things in, or delicates, as she had called them. The upper half was a mirror that was bracketed on both sides with more windows. These were high enough that they didn't need the privacy of shutters to keep anyone from looking in. The wall closest to the bedroom was narrow. It had a dresser at the back and as far back as Cait could remember, had held night gowns and a few robes. Also, it held the extra towels, and other linens. The white commode was right inside the door from the small hall. But the center of the room held the tub. It was a doublewide claw footed one that had a shower curtain that surrounded the tub. Cait had never known anyone to use the bath as a shower, but it was there all the same.

The bedroom was about the same size as the bath with the only difference being the closet. This room had a very large one that, when they came to visit, would fill with things Aunt Dee would purchase to take back with them at the end of her stay. The bed had been her mother's mother's and she'd had to have a mattress made for it when it had needed replacing since it was so big. The four posters and the small stairs used to get into it were made of mahogany and the wood shone with the love and pride that had been lovingly stroked into it with each polishing. There was no other furniture in the room aside from the rocking chair that sat next to the fireplace and the huge cabinet that held her aunt's dolls.

There were hundreds of them, from a very small two inches high to about three feet. She had told Cait once that she hadn't brought them to the United States with her because she wanted to leave them in their home and she had family there when she came to visit.

The kitchen was smallish, not having the need to cook for many people; Aunt Dee had never seen a reason to expand the little room. It did have modern fixtures, a microwave and convection oven. The window over the double sink looked over the back yard and a massive herb garden. When Cait had gone into the kitchen for a glass of water, she noticed that the garden had been well maintained while they had been away. There was a small table in the kitchen and around it were three chairs. The cabinets, all glass fronted, were a beautiful oak and carried the same stamp of love the rest of the house did.

The living room, the room where Cait sat, was the best room in the house. There wasn't a couch, but four overstuffed chairs that faced the fireplace. Between each chair there was a tall reading lamp that stood next to a table. On either side of the fireplace were bookcases filled with an eclectic amount of books, paperback and hard back both. This room, like all the others, had hardwood floors made of parquet, even the bath. The walls were white in here, which was good as the rooms colors were tossed about the room like a painter's palate, mostly earth tones, but with an occasional bright green or pink too. She was just getting up to turn down the flames when someone knocked at her door.

"Hello, missus. I'm Shamus Flanagan from town. My wife and I take care of the house for you whilst you and your'n are away. I was wondering if everything was to suit you? The missus and I, we've been wondering also how yer holding up. We was powerful sorry to hear about Deidra. She was a wonderment, she was."

"Yes. Yes, Mr. Flanagan, everything is fine. I thank you for...my aunt always said she never had to concern herself about the house knowing that you were here. I thank you for it. She left the house...she left it to me when she was...when she passed. I sent her here, did you know?"

"Aye, we all turned out for her funeral. Too bad you couldn't attend. Beautiful, it was. I hear tell you've been...if you don't mind my saying, you look a little worn out yourself. You sure you should be out and about?"

Cait smiled. She was sure she had horrified the man when she opened the door for him. "Yes. I'm fine. I've come to...I have to clean things up and I'm...do you know of a family that might need somewhere to live? It would have to be a small family, of course."

"You were planning to rent it out? Well, my youngest, he is wedding soon. Could maybe take it off'n your hands. For the right price, that is. You have a rent in mind?"

"I'm sure it will suit him. What's his name?" Cait did not elaborate on what she was going to do with the house, letting him think what he wanted.

"Shawn. His new bride will be Leona. She's a foreigner like yourself, an American. I'll send him by to you to interview sometime. You let me know when you're feeling up to it."

"Mr. Flanagan, maybe he could...do you think he could drive me around a bit? I can rent a car for him if he doesn't have one. I want to...I need to talk to my aunt." She flushed, afraid he would think she was crazy for wanting to talk to her dead aunt, but he seemed to understand.

"You just leave it to me, missus. Shawn will be here tomorrow if'n you think you'll be ready. He has a lorry and it will get you there in some comfort."

She agreed and he set off. She hobbled back over to the chair and sat down. She realized she should have invited him in and felt bad for not doing so. Snuggling down into her chair, she cried herself to sleep.

~~~

Cait got up at two o'clock in the morning, the time change and sleeping in the chair waking her. She looked around the room and decided to get going. There was a lot to be done and she just wanted it done.

Starting in the bedroom, she began taking things out of the closet, which was not much, and sorting them out. She didn't know why she started in the hardest room for her, but figured maybe it had to do with getting the hard part over first. The packing boxes she had had delivered had been put in all the rooms she had asked, along with all the box tape and bubble wrap. She put all the clothes in the bedroom and the bath into four big boxes and marked them, charity. She didn't strip the bed yet, knowing she would take a nap sometime before Shawn showed up at noon.

The bath was next. This room was where her aunt had put on her talc, and the smell brought her to tears. When Cait had found the small poof, she held it to her face and sobbed like a baby. There were a few things in this room she put aside for a box to go to the United States.

At eleven-thirty, she had everything packed and marked for where they were to go. It had taken longer because she had to move around on the crutch she had to use because of her leg.

The cabinets were all empty and there was only a jug of water in the fridge and her glass on the counter.

Her gun, a small revolver, she put on the counter with some stationary she had found in the bedroom. Everything else had been either put into boxes or into the trash barrel out from the house. She was putting a tag on the vacuum cleaner when Shawn arrived.

~CHAPTER TWENTY-FIVE~

Spencer's plane landed at nine that same morning. He and his mom and Meggie had been on a plane for the past fourteen hours and he was exhausted. It had taken everything he had in him not to sob with joy at being this much closer to Cait. By eleven, they were in their hotel.

Nicky and Devin had worked for two days to figure out where Cait had been taken. And he wouldn't have been sure they had figured it out if Donald had not mentioned that Aunt Dee had arrived in Ireland just fine when he had stopped by one day for a beer. Spencer still chuckled when he thought of the captain trying to not give anything away while giving them all the necessary information they needed.

"Yeah. The funeral home in Shelton, Ireland said they received the casket just fine. Said she'd be laid to rest in Shelton, Ireland on Tuesday morning. Ever been to Ireland? Me either, but I think if I were going to visit, I'd be heading to Shelton, Ireland."

"Is there an airport in Shelton, Captain?"

Spencer looked at Nicky, confused. Why should he care if there was an airport? Did he think Aunt Dee was going to take flying lessons? Then he looked at the captain again.

"Holy shit!" Finally getting it, Spencer stood up. "She's in Ireland."

Donald shook his head, finished his beer, and left.

Within ten minutes, Spencer had booked three seats on the next plane out. Dan stayed to keep the boys in school for their last few weeks and his mom decided to go to help care for Meggie while he went to convince Cait to come back with him.

The little hotel they were booked in was beautiful. Meggie, never one to be shy, went to play with the owner's grandchildren in the back yard while his mother took a nap. Spencer sat in one of the outdoor chairs and watched her while the owner's son, Daniel Taylor, tried to explain to him how to get to the O'Malley house.

"Dinna think anyone was coming this year, what with the funeral and all. Missus O'Malley will surely be missed. My momma loved her dearly; they went to school together. The whole town turned out for her wake. I hear tell Paddy had a policeman's honor. He was a good man too."

"Yes, he was. I'm actually here to see Caitlynne. Do you know if she's staying there or not? The hospital said that's where they thought she'd go after she had been released."

"Oh, aye. My uncle Shawn, he's the caretaker for the house when they don't be in town. He said she called the other day and had them bring out some food and such. Aye, she's there."

When Daniel offered to take him up to the house, Spencer could have leapt for joy. He felt a compelling need to see her that he could not explain. After his mother woke up and agreed to keep an eye on Meggie, he was off again.

Spencer was nervous when they stopped in front of the little house. He couldn't seem to make himself move. What if she told him to fuck off, which he had no doubt that she would, but he had already decided that he was not going to give up. He loved her and needed her.

"You can go on in. There isn't a lock on the door — never needed one around here. Shamus won't have come back yet, or he'd be parked here in the turnout. It's a fair piece to the cemetery and back." Daniel had called his uncle to see if he had heard of Miss Caitlynne having plans for the day and he had told them that she was going up to talk to her Aunt Dee. If'n you need a ride back to the hotel, just give me a call. Just tell Mary Katherine to connect you to the hotel; she'll know the number."

Spencer got out and walked up to the porch. He was amazed at the riot of colors in the flower beds out front and along the sides of the house. He tried the door knob and when it turned easily enough, he turned and waved Daniel off.

There were boxes everywhere. All marked with one thing or another. The house felt...well, empty, he supposed, and realized that except for the few pieces of heavy furniture, it was. He pulled out is cell phone and called his mom to tell her that he had made it and that she was not home.

"I bet it's a lovely house, out there in the heather fields. Mrs. Taylor said that an O'Malley has lived in this town since the early twelfth century. She said that it's tiny, though, not big enough for a family."

"Yeah, it's tiny. But it probably seems smaller because of all the boxes. It looks like she's been busy. Everything is all...huh, there's a box here with Meggie's name on it." He wanted to open it, but didn't know what Cait would think if he did. She was mad enough at him already.

"Meggie?" He was surprised at the tone and dreaded what she had meant by it. "Spencer, look around the house and tell me what you see. All the rooms, even the bath, I want you to pull back the curtain and look."

"Mom? What is it? I can hear the concern and worry in your voice."

"Just look for me. Tell me what's in the bath. Are there towels hanging up, any soap or shampoo in the dish?"

"No. Nothing. Mom, your worrying me now. The bed is stripped and there are no linens in the room. She's probably already packed them to leave. Her things are packed too. Maybe she was coming home, you think?" When she didn't answer, Spencer's heart started to pound.

"What's in the kitchen? The refrigerator? Anything in the cabinets?" she asked instead.

"No, a jug of water in the fridge and a glass on the counter, and nothing else. Mom, what is it, what are you thinking?"

"Spencer, I hope I'm wrong, but I don't think Caitlynne is coming home. I think, oh dear, I hope I'm wrong, but I think she's gone there to kill herself. I've been around enough of these types of cases when the living relative of a tragic loss feels that they are to blame. And we both know that's what she's feeling. Look at how she went in to get Meggie—seemingly without fear. And that nice young boy, what did he say his uncle said? That she was looking for someone to take the house? Oh, son, she can't do this; you can't let her."

"I won't, Mom. I'll...she won't." Spencer closed his phone and sat on the sheet-covered chair.

He knew his mother was right. And this was his fault. He had driven her to this point by blaming her for Meggie's kidnapping. And what had she said to Donald? That she was sorry Meggie had been hurt. Like she it was her fault. Damn it all to hell.

He didn't know how long he had been sitting there when he heard a vehicle pull up. He stood and started for the door, but was afraid if she saw him, she would bolt again. Spencer needed her where he could hold her. And beat her ass if she did not listen to him.

Spencer waited until he heard the car pulling away, the sound of the engine growing faint. He stepped out the door to her house when he heard her crutches on the steps.

"Hello, O'Malley. How's it going?"

~~~

Cait nearly fell backward, and might have if Spencer hadn't grabbed her. It felt so good to be in his arms that she swayed into his warmth. Then she pulled back and did fall.

"Damn it, woman. What the hell is the matter with you?" When he picked her up as if she weighted nothing at all, she didn't think to object to being carted around until they were in the house and he had her laid on the bed.

"What the hell are...how did you...you are going back where you came from right this instant. I did not ask you here."

"Why?"

That threw her. She just stared at him opened mouth. Why indeed? she thought.

"Because I said so. Now...now, you just go. I have things...what are you doing here anyway? You know, I don't care. Leave." She started to stand and he pushed her back on the bed. When she lifted her crutch still clutched in her hand, he took it from her and tossed it across the room.

"This is how things are going to go from now on. You will listen to me, and before you get all pissy with me, I said listen to me, not obey." He started taking off his shirt and when it was unbuttoned, he tossed it to the floor. "That's not to say that I won't want you to obey, but as a matter of course, I'll hope you will."

"What...why are you getting undressed? You can't...you need to leave right now, Grant. I have things to do."

"I'm getting undressed because I'm going to make love with you. And I find that much more enjoyable when we are both naked. And what were your plans for this evening, O'Malley? You're not going anywhere; you don't have a car. You've packed everything up. Tell me, love, what where you planning?" He took off his belt and tossed it near the shirt. Cait watched it as it slithered open and lay flat.

"You can't. You have to...please don't do this. I need to...please, Spencer. You don't know how hard...I...they're all dead because of me. My mother, my uncle, and aunt. I couldn't even...someone hit Meggie." Tears streamed down her face and she tried to turn away from him and huddle into the bed.

His heart hurt for her. He gathered her up into his arms and pulled her into his lap, much in the same way he did Meggie when she needed comfort. He held her as she cried her sobs and tears poured from her. When she finally settled, he held her still.

"Meggie is with me—she and my mom. We arrived today and I came straight here to talk to you. My mom, I was on the phone with her when I looked around and she told me...she knew that you that you...O'Malley, I love you. I've never loved anyone as much as I do you. I can't...I can't tell you how sorry I am that I hurt you." When she shifted in his arms, he let her lean back, but he didn't release her.

"Hurt me? How did you...? You didn't hurt me. I let those men take her. I'm the one who—"

"No you didn't. O'Malley, for a very smart woman, you are fairly stupid when you want to be, aren't you? Did you hand Meggie over to them? No, you fought them with all you had. Did you make your aunt and uncle fight with you? No, you did not. Do you think had you have told them to stay safe inside the house they would have? I'm sure you know as well as I do that they wouldn't have. And had that been your uncle or aunt, you wouldn't have either. No, families help each other, and that's what they did. You got Meggie back for me, yes. But I believe you love her as much as I do and got her for you as well."

"Of course I love her. And I'm not stupid. I caused this whole thing because I should have stayed in Chicago and then none of you would have been hurt. Ouch! That hurt."

He rubbed her bottom where he had just swatted her, and looked down at her. "Unless you want me to do that again, I would strongly suggest that you stop that kind of logic right now. If you had stayed, I would never have fallen in love with you. Now, enough talk. I want you naked in two minutes or there will be hell to pay."

"There are no sheets out. I've packed them all and I'm not having sex with you. You still need to..."

He covered her mouth with his. Her lips were soft and warm and when he nipped at her lower lip, gently, careful of the stitches, she opened for him. Her tongue slid along his in a sensual duel and when he felt her arms go up around his neck, he adjusted her so that he could stretch her out on the bed beneath him.

He knew that making love with her would be a challenge; she had one hand in a cast and her leg in another from her thigh to her knee. Her lip was still swollen and both her eyes were darkened with bruises. He thought she was the most beautiful thing he had ever seen. When he pulled away and stood, he wanted to grab scissors and cut her clothing away rather than try to remove them.

There were several boxes in this room and he opened the first one he came to and found the linens. After pulling out towels and pillowcases, he finally found sheets. When he turned around to put them on the bed, Cait was sitting up and unbuttoning her shirt. He watched, the sheets completely forgotten in his hand.

"Are you going to put the bed together, or watch me undress?"

He looked at her, thinking that was by and far the dumbest question she had ever asked him. Watching her was much better than making a bed they were just going to mess up anyway.

"Okay, let me rephrase that. If you want to see anymore of me, then you'd better get the bed made."

He snapped out of his stupor and advanced toward her and the bed. She had already unlaced the soft cast on her thigh and it lay limp around her ankle and foot. She shimmied her pants down and let them hang there as well. He couldn't see what she had on under her shirt as she had not taken it off yet.

"I think I can manage both if you do it very slowly. I love to watch you peel off the layers that hid you from me. Leave on your bra and panties for me. I want to take them...Christ, O'Malley." He hissed, his voice full of sharp pain.

She had no bra on. Her breasts bounced gently when she flipped her shirt over to where his lay. He had to stop trying to get the fitted sheet over the mattress and adjust his cock before he hurt himself. Then thinking he would be more comfortable, he unsnapped them and pulled them off, briefs and all.

His cock, hard and thick, stood straight from his groin and the harder Cait stared at him, the harder and achier he got. Her groan nearly had him leap across the bed and throw her down and take her. When she licked her lips and bent over to remove the cast and her pants from the bottom half of her leg, he looked at the mirror just behind her on the bathroom door.

Spencer could see her tight curls wet with her need and her thighs damp with her arousal. When she winked at him in the reflection, he fisted his cock and walked toward her.

"You are going to pay for teasing me, O'Malley. I'm going to make you wait until you are out of your mind with need before I let you come. Then I'm going to do it again and again until you can't stand up." He flicked the sheet over the ends of the mattress and slid up behind her.

When she stood up, her back pressing hard against his front, he reached around and cupped her breasts. Her nipples, pink and hard, rolled between his fingers and she moved her ass against his cock.

"Please, Grant. I've missed your body touching mine. I want you to take me this way, but I don't think I can stand that long. Please."

He knew she was right; her leg had not healed enough and he didn't want her to be in pain. Picking her up gently with his arm around her waist, he guided them both to the bed. When they were close, he turned her around, leaned down, and took one of her pert nipples into his mouth and nibbled. Her hand on his shoulder gripped him tightly.

Spencer picked her up and laid her down on the bed. He stood over her and looked at her. When she started to cover her wounds, still red and raw, he stopped her by pulling her hand down to her side.

"Never cover yourself from me, O'Malley. These scars mean that you come home to me. I don't see them. All I see is you, and I love you."

He moved to his pants, reached into the pocket, and pulled out what he wanted. Moving to the foot of the bed, he knelt between her open legs and smiled. She was his, finally.

Running his hands up her thighs and to her juncture, he feathered his fingers along her muscles and back again. Her shuddering breath told him she was enjoying his touch and he did it again. Leaning forward, still on his knees, he nipped at her hip bone, first on the left, then on the right. On his way back across her, he whorled his tongue deep into her belly button and bit her there as well.

Kissing his way down her body, he spread her legs wide and put her non-injured leg over his shoulder as he settled between her legs, his mouth mere inches from paradise. He spread her nether lips open and stared at the glistening pink flesh and the hard nub hidden there. Licking his lips, he leaned in and swiped his tongue from her gate to her clit. She groaned and lifted her hips for more.

He wanted to make her suffer, but found that he would, as well, and wanted to make her come and drink from her when she did. Opening his mouth over her clit and his tongue in her pussy, he slid two fingers deep into her and fucked her like he wanted to with his cock. Cait filled his mouth with her honey, hot, spicy and his.

When he added a third finger, he nipped at her and she screamed. Not a dainty cry of release, a full out scream. Spencer suckled and licked as his fingers filled her. Over and over, she ground her pussy against his tongue.

Moving up her body, he kissed her ribs, the bruises and the cuts. When he got to her breasts, he kissed the wounds there and licked her nipple until it was a hard peak and stood tight for him. With another lick, he swirled his tongue over it again and watched as it seemed to beg for his mouth. Spencer dropped the ring over her hard nipple from his mouth as he entered her and stopped moving. When she looked up at him, he nodded to the ring.

"Marry me, O'Malley. If you answer me correctly, I'll move again." He kissed her other breast as she stared at him.

"Now you blackmail me? Grant, please, fuck me. I'll...oh, please. I'll answer you later. I want...I need to come with you."

"No, an answer now, O'Malley, or I pull out and leave you hanging. Will. You. Marry. Me? A simple yes will end this."

She tried to move, but he was too heavy for her. When she started tightening her muscles along her channel, he thought he might be in trouble, but he shifted and pushed forward and she moaned again.

"Answer me, baby. Answer me and I'll finish us both."

For a few more seconds, she bit her lip and refused to answer and he surged forward just enough to make her moan then stopped again.

"Yes. Yes. Yes, please, Grant, please yes, I'll marry you. Please." She sobbed at him and he pulled out to the tip and surged forward hard — once, twice, on the third push into her, she arched up and came. When she clutched him, her muscles pulling and milking him, he came as well, his seed filling her as he poured into her heat.

He dropped down on her shoulder and then rolled to the side, grabbing the ring as he went. He pulled her left hand down and kissed her finger and slid the ring onto it.

"I love you, O'Malley. You've made me the happiest man in the world. And I will love you more every day for the rest of our lives."

~CHAPTER TWENTY-SIX~

Cait was standing in the back of the church surrounded by what seemed like the entire town. She knew all the people in the room, her two new sisters-in-law — at least by the end of the day they would be — Ben Kendal, who had designed her dress and made it for her, her future mother-in-law and her husband Dan, and Meggie.

Cait looked down at Meggie. She had not looked happy all day and Cait sat on the couch next to her, much to the horror of Ben who had been fluffing her butt for over an hour.

The dress was beautiful. The white silk fit her long, slim frame like a glove, hugging her curves and waist like Ben had painted it on her. At the back, over her butt, was a large taffeta bow that held the long train to the dress. Once she and Spencer were married and at the reception hall, the train and bow would come off and she would be allow to sit like a normal person again. The top of the dress was sheer silk that draped over her shoulders and hid her scars on her chest. The long sleeves buttoned at the wrist and finished at the elbow. She had asked Ben to put as many buttons on the dress as he could and he had refused.

"What's up, kiddo? Don't you like your dress? I think you look prettier than I do, if you want the truth."

"No, it's pretty. I even like my shoes, but I don't want to be flower girl. I want to be something else."

"Well, baby, what is it you want to be? I'll do everything I can to make you happy today because when you're sad, I'm sad."

When Meggie explained what she wanted, Cait smiled. Then she laughed. Oh yeah, she thought, she could make this happen. She pulled out her cell phone to text Spencer.

"U trust me? I wnt to mke last min change to ceremony."

"R u still marrying me?"

"Yes."

"Then don't care. Change away."

"I love u."

"I love u 2"

Next, Cait pulled Dan aside and told him what she wanted. Smiling down at Meggie, she winked. Things were about to be fun.

~~~

When Spencer and his brothers were told it was time, he snapped his phone closed and they all walked out into the church. It was time and he was excited to see what Cait had done.

When the music started and he looked down the aisle, he nearly laughed out loud. Coming down the aisle was Dan dressed in his tux with a ridiculously small basket in his hand tossing rose petals at the guests. He was laughing so hard he had to lean against a pew at one point to catch his breath. The congregation was enjoying the change as well, everyone in the spirit with him. The ring bearer, a son of one of Cait's friends, kept looking at Dan as if he was afraid he was going to get into trouble and he wanted no part of it. When they made it to the front, Dan reached out and hugged Spencer tight and then stepped back.

The six bridesmaids were next, each of them dressed in policeman blue dresses with a bouquet of lilies and roses. Both flowers had been favorites of Cait's aunt and uncle. When the wedding march started and Cait came around the corner, it took him a moment to realize who was giving her away.

Meggie was holding her hand and smiling as big as he had ever seen her. He didn't know where the tiny veil she had on had come from, but she, too, was dressed like the bride — white dresses and all.

When the women in his life got to the front of the church, the minister cleared his throat and Cait stepped up and whispered in his ear. When he nodded and cleared his throat again, Spencer looked at his bride.

"Ladies and gentlemen, there is going to be a small change in the ceremony. If you could all just bear with us for just a moment, then I'm sure you'll understand. Miss O'Malley."

Cait dropped to the floor and turned Meggie to face her. Cait looked into the audience and smiled at his mother. "Mrs. Parker, could you please stand behind me and help me? I want Meggie to understand everything I say to her, but I need both hands. Please?"

"Sure, if you will please stop calling me Mrs. Parker. I swear, girl, you're going to be my daughter in a few minutes and I'd like to be called Margaret, please." She was moving out into the aisle as she spoke and was soon standing behind Cait.

Suddenly, Cait stood, turned around and hugged his mom. Spencer was not sure what was said, but his mother started crying and hugged her back. After a few more minutes of the two of them whispering to each other, Cait turned back around and sat before Meggie, her face red from crying. Taking a ring off a necklace at her neck, Cait kissed Meggie.

"Megan Shannon Grant, with this ring, I make you my daughter. And from this day forward, you will be mine as much as your daddy will be too. I will love you and care for you in sickness and in health. I will honor you and hold you when you need me to. I will not give you space when I know you need a hug, and I'll spank you bottom when you piss...err when you need it. By taking this ring, you will always, no matter what, have a place in my heart and I will love you and I will always be there for you. I love you, Meggie."

Spencer heard his brother Damon sniffle and then another brother blow his nose. Looking at his mother, she was crying in earnest and wiping the tears away as Dan held her close. Everyone in the church, including the minister, was openly crying at the pair on the floor. When Meggie nodded and held out her hand, Cait slipped the ring on her finger and they hugged.

"Okay, Rev, we're finished. You can hitch us now," Cait said as she stood again, holding Meggie's hand.

Spencer reached out, pulled Cait to him, and kissed her. Then he reached down and picked up his daughter, their daughter, and nodded to the minister too. His family was ready and he knew for as long as he lived, this would be the one moment in time that he would never forget.

ABOUT THE AUTHOR

I woke up one morning and decided to give play time to the people in my head who were keeping me awake. Little did I know that they would be so relentless and want their time right now! I wrote for the pure joy of it and to entertain my family and friends. But mostly it was to get more than an hour of sleep without a story playing out. Of course, the more I write, the more they want. So…well, as a result of sleepless days (I work through the night as a gun toting grandma – nope not a vigilantly but an armed security guard) I have lots of stories written.

Hello! My name is Kathi Barton and I'm an author. I have been married to my very best friend Sonny for at times seems several lifetimes – in a good way, honey. And together we have three wonderful children and then the ones we brought into the world - Paul and Dale Barton, Jason and Wendy Barton and Danielle and Ben Conklin. They have given us seven of the greatest treasures on Earth. They don't live at home seven days a week! No, seriously, seven grandchildren – Gavin, Spring, Ben, Trinity, Sarah, Kelly and Kian.

www.ingramcontent.com/pod-product-compliance
Lightning Source LLC
Chambersburg PA
CBHW020557180626
46810CB00007B/2546